PRAISE FOR STEPHEN DAISL

WINNER, Prime Minister's Liter

WINNER, UTS Glenda Adams Award for New Writing,
NSW Premier's Literary Awards 2011

Shortlisted, WA Premier's Book Award for Fiction, 2011

Shortlisted, Commonwealth Writers Prize for Best First Book 2011
(South-east Asia and Pacific Region)

Shortlisted, Christina Stead Prize for Fiction,
NSW Premier's Literary Awards 2011

'Stephen Daisley's *Traitor* is one of the finest debut novels
I have read. Indeed it's one of the best novels I have read
in recent years....I want to add it to the list of great modern
novels about war...And it's about so much more than
war: love, friendship, loyalty, honour, mercy, spirituality,
multiculturalism, class. It's a work of emotional depth;
perhaps the sort of book you can only write in middle age.'
Stephen Romei, *Australian*

'Suffused with love, beauty and loneliness. The creation and
development of the character of David Monroe is masterful,
not least because he is a man of so few words. Also impressive is
Daisley's control of structure...His book is a revelation, woven
as delicately as Monroe's precious prayer rug. A rare pleasure.'
Australian Literary Review

'A bold debut and a unique story...Winton-esque dialogue.'
Australian Bookseller & Publisher

'Strangely existential, achingly personal, irritatingly poetic, you'll
love it or hate it—or love and hate it all at once.' *GQ Australia*

'Terrific debut...Exquisitely crafted and beautifully written.'
Sunday Star Times NZ

'Stephen Daisley's debut novel is one of beautiful contrasts…
Daisley's greatest success in this novel is the depiction
of a simple man with great depth.' *Age*

'A beautifully sparse portrayal—the emotional toll of a
soldier's past choices symbolised by the reticent and
isolated figure is palpable. His is an unusually nuanced
examination of heroism and love.' *Sun Herald*

'Impact galore. His descriptions of Monroe's life as a station
shepherd and his relationship with the few people, as well as
animals, within his ken are superb. But that adjective applies to
the entire essence of the novel…The taut style delivers narrative
which is striking and suffused with reminders of life's fragilities.
The few characters are well drawn. It is likely that much more
will be heard of Daisley…He has the sure touch of a highly
gifted storyteller.' *Otago Daily Times*

'A confident and haunting exploration of the nature of betrayal…
Daisley's confident handling of the complex chronology is a
major strength, as is his command of narrative. The account
of trench warfare is imaginative and finely detailed. All signal
the debut of an important new talent.' *Listener* NZ

Stephen Daisley was born in 1955 and grew up in the North Island
of New Zealand. He has worked on sheep and cattle stations, on
oil and gas construction sites and as a truck driver, among many
other jobs.

He lives in Western Australia with his wife and five children.

Stephen
Daisley
Coming
Rain

TEXT PUBLISHING MELBOURNE AUSTRALIA

textpublishing.com.au

The Text Publishing Company
Swann House
22 William Street
Melbourne Victoria 3000
Australia

First published in 2015 by The Text Publishing Company

Cover design by W. H. Chong
Page design by Text
Typeset in Adobe Caslon Pro by J & M Typesetting

Printed and bound in Australia by Griffin Press, an Accredited ISO AS/NZS 14001:2004 Environmental Management System printer

National Library of Australia Cataloguing-in-Publication entry:
Creator: Daisley, Stephen, author.
Title: Coming rain / by Stephen Daisley.
ISBN: 9781922182029 (paperback)
             9781925095029 (ebook)
Subjects: Country life—Western Australia—Fiction.
             Agricultural laborers—Western Australia—Fiction.
Dewey Number: A823.4

This book is printed on paper certified against the Forest Stewardship Council® Standards. Griffin Press holds FSC chain-of-custody certification SGS-COC-005088. FSC promotes environmentally responsible, socially beneficial and economically viable management of the world's forests.

This project has been assisted by the Commonwealth Government through the Australia Council, its arts funding and advisory body.

To Sylvia

The father...lit the candle at the kitchen fire, put it where it shouldn't light the boy's face, and watched him. And the child knew he was watching him, and pretended to sleep, and, so pretending, he slept.

HENRY LAWSON
'A Child in the Dark, and a Foreign Father'

The dingo ran as if she had been here forever. Loose jointed, her tongue wet and long and eyes nonchalant as she travelled. Ears forward and nose taking in the river of yonga grey coming to her as she crossed a clearing and paused among karrik bush. Looked back to where she had come from.

The last of the day's sun and the first of the four moons rising above the bloodwoods. The grey kangaroo, upwind of her, grazing quietly across a long, flat valley fringed with desert oak. They were deliberate, selecting and nibbling the beardy grasses. Their slow, graceful feeding in the twilight. They moved through saltbush and into a grove of long-leaf paperbarks.

The bitch flattened, laid her ears back and watched. She lifted her nose to the horizon and the last of the sun lines, second moon coming. If she was to have meat this night she would need to act immediately.

She came out of the smoke bush slowly at first, then sprinting to close on the mob, and was among them. Ranged alongside, watching their panic as she harried them, searching out what she wanted.

A young doe carrying nyarnyee in her pouch collided with balga, a little grass tree, and lost her footing. She rolled over and righted. The face and front feet of the nyarnyee came out of the pouch. The mother seemed to stand on her head as she aligned herself, saving her baby. She turned and bounded desperately behind the scattering mob. The dingo raced to flank them. They veered from her and she dropped back to make her kill. The mother with the nyarnyee still lagging behind the main mob, frantic to catch up. The dingo closed and balanced again, turned into the run of the yonga, her head towards the long throat; laid her ears back and launched into her killing attack.

The wide-eyed kangaroo flung herself away to the left, skittering through paperbarks; paused in the long grass and shook her head as if to get her bearings. It was another few seconds before she seemed to register where she was and turned to follow her clan.

The dingo somersaulted when she fell, rolling over and over in the dirt. She lay on the ground, her sides heaving. Then she sat up, closed her mouth and stood. Circled the droppings and urine, rubbed her face and neck in the scat and rolled over in it; shook, got to her feet and gave a barking howl; listened to the yonga leaping through the brush. Their strong scent, like water, an easy path for her to follow.

It was just dark when she closed on them again. The third moon three-quarters high and bright. This time it was in open ground, a man-made clearing, a road and prickly dryandra bushes. The yonga nervous now along the verge between the bushes, tentatively grazing on new grass. Again they smelled and heard her, gave off the loud clicks and bounded away. She feinted left to bunch them and just as quickly swung to the right flank to turn them into heavier scrub, all the time searching out the mother carrying the nyarnyee.

It was then that the headlights came on down the road. Great yellow white lights running through the night.

She immediately abandoned her hunt, turned from the monstrous presence and ran at a sharp angle from the road into the scrub. As she ran, there was a great thump. The terrible lights colliding with her prey. She stopped, lay down and waited; listening to the voices. One of the lights had gone out. Men were talking to each other through the trees. Young man, old man. She saw dust rise through the remaining light and clouds crossing the moon. It was silent for a long time before she approached where the noise had come from. Almost morning. Sister sun coming up.

Lew saw the woman walking out of the ocean at Cottesloe Beach. She was bending forward, scooping up handfuls of sea water and throwing them in front of herself. This fine woman staring at him, at his big hands, white arms and body whipped with cuts from the thorns, saltbush and spinifex. Christ.

Another set of waves came in, pushing her up and forward, and she lifted her arms and elbows to keep balance. Stepped out of the water. The tide was being sucked back into the ocean, stripping the sand from beneath her feet. The constant sound of the small waves breaking on the beach. He was just twenty-one and couldn't swim.

She put her head to one side and removed the rubber swimming cap. Damp brown hair fell to her shoulders. 'Do you want something?'

The black woollen costume had gathered close into her and sea water was running down between her legs. Instead of speaking, he looked away to the shark-net pylon in the sea. A boy, long armed, up on the concrete shoulder, holding the iron pole. Another crouched to dive off. They were black against the sky.

Someone was calling from the new car park. 'Is that you down there? Young Mr McCleod?' He called Lew's name as if he was announcing a runner in the Melbourne Cup.

An older man, barefoot, walking awkwardly across the white sand. He raised a hand to block the sun.

Lew waved at him. A smile broke out on his face. 'Painter. Here, mate.'

The old man approaching them was wearing a blue Jackie Howe shearers singlet. Unshaved face. A bald head worn brown in the sun, covered in scars and odd bumps. Both ears were lumped, cauliflowered, and his left ear was much smaller. The nose broken so many times there was no bridge left. He had big wrinkled hands covered in tattoos of birds and stars. Strong, don't touch me arms, veins stood in his biceps. Spider webs on both elbows. Forearms showed thick blue outlines of a ship in full sail and a naked woman in high heels with her hands behind her head, elbows like a bottle opener. Mary. A heart with an arrow through it.

His name was Painter Hayes and he was squinting at them in the glare of the sunlight coming off the sand. Opened his mouth to smile. 'Jesus this sand is hot. And white as you like. Go blind,' he said.

The woman in the woollen bathing costume spoke to him. 'How do you do?'

Painter nodded to her. 'Not bad. You?'

She stepped back. 'Fine, thank you.'

'Why did we come here again, son?' Painter, lowering his

voice. Speaking to Lew but he kept looking at her.

'For a swim.' Lew folded his arms. A muscle in his jaw flexed.

'That surf patrol is marching over here like they want to rescue someone and they not fuckin' singin' come to me Jesus neither,' Painter said and looked away to his left. 'They got ropes on their heads before. Walking about the show like they own the fuckin' place.' He touched his nose with his thumb. Nodded to say I see you there and sorry missus, I know. I know, the language. Wide strong wrists he had. Shearer's wrists. Fighter's hands.

Lew reached out his hand towards her to introduce himself. He had found his voice in the apology and presence of the other man. 'My name is Lewis McCleod. I'm a shearer. We just got in from Mrs Anderson Darcy's place, been shearing the rams. Me and Painter Hayes here. Tupping soon, that's why the rams now see.' Sorry about him. Look at me. He's not right in the head.

She said nothing, looking at him as if he was a lunatic. Would not take his hand.

He kept speaking. 'Lot of them thorny bloody Merinos covered in the spinifex and saltbush. All through the wool, the wrinkly-necked bastards. Cut you apart.'

The water had stopped running off her. She watched him, and still did not accept his introduction. 'You came down for a swim?'

'I did. Came down, didn't expect to see you. Never been here before.'

She was nodding. 'Mrs Anderson Darcy's? Tupping?'

'Son,' Painter said. 'Come on, we better go. Stop talking to her. Oh no, look out, they're here.'

Three muscular young men stood there with their arms folded over their chests. Their feet firmly in the white beach sand. Red and yellow skullcaps on their heads tied up under the chin with strings.

'What are you doing here?' one of the lifeguards asked. His face all red. White zinc on his nose.

Lew pointed at the ocean.

'Maureen,' a lifeguard said. 'Don't talk to these blokes. They are just no-hopers. They don't even belong here. Look at them.'

Painter spoke to the red-faced man. 'We were just leaving. On our way, come on son cut it out. I never been to the bloody beach in me life. You neither. Fuckin' beach, Mr Jesus where are you now? Why would you want to lie out in the sand anyway? Fuckin' cook.'

'Watch your mouth old man,' one of the lifesavers said. 'There is a lady present and this is not a sewer.'

Painter glanced at him and nodded.

'No no,' Lew said. 'Now hold on a minute mate.' Wide shoulders turning.

Maureen sniffed, shrugged and looked back to the ocean. 'I don't know.'

Groups of bathers had stopped splashing and were standing still, staring at them. Blue-and-white striped beach umbrellas tilted towards the sun. Frowning mothers holding up towels and little children running to them with chubby, outstretched arms. The pylon divers also stopped and were looking in their direction, leaning out to one side, holding the pole.

Painter looked at Lew. 'Don't,' he said. 'I mean it son, don't. Oh no.'

Lew stepped forward and pushed the lifeguard who had been speaking to him.

'Fuck off.'

The lifeguard fell back and another lifeguard ran in and shoulder-charged Lew. 'Fair bump, play on,' he yelled, turned and snarled.

Lew fell backwards into the sand. He was playing football.

Now they were fighting.

Lew was on his back, arms and legs waving like an upturned turtle. He was trying to get up. Somebody else stood above him and swung both fists at his head. Hit him on the cheekbone once and in the mouth, forehead and nose. He saw Painter stepping over and pushing away the man who had been punching his face. There was a roaring of voices as the old man moved forward and knocked one of the surf rescue blokes down. Turned as he was hit from behind; covered up, blocked and hit another with a combination of punches. Old man moving like a good fighter, sound as a bell of brass but step into your punches son and no cursing nor profanity when you box I will not have it, the old trainer Mr Kilpatrick speaking to him yet. Fine fine…but keep your hands up and be aware of yourself as you move above the canvas; did you hear me, above and not on or about the canvas? You come to bearing close to the gentleman Mr Eagan, the American Irish…A prince in the ring and no doubt about it.

Two straight rights double jab, step-away left hook and down goes another lifesaver on his red and yellow arse. Painter blew air and snot from what was left of his nose and danced to his left, hands up. 'Yep. That'll do. Good. Wait on now boys. My hands are not what they were and I need to see them.' He coughed and his bottom lip rode up onto his top lip for a moment. He allowed it and pulled his chin in. Waved his right hand up and down as if in pain; all the time he studied them. 'Hurts.'

'You ugly old bastard,' one of the lifesavers said. Fingers holding his bleeding nose, bent over and backing away. 'You just broke my nose.'

'You got any wet paper bags boys?' Painter, smiling. 'I couldn't punch me way out of one if you paid me. Not a single one. Would you ever look at me? Knackered. Old as a rock.'

Lew on all fours, blood streaming from his nose and mouth and about to stand. Becoming giddy and still seeing white sand kicking up. Got to his feet, staggered to one side. Noticed the woman Maureen had walked off a few yards, folded her arms and was watching them all.

'Run, son,' Painter says to him over his shoulder, 'go on now, get on up out of it.'

Lew began running in the soft white sand, paused and looked back.

Painter had stepped away from the lifesavers and was once again appealing to them. 'Come on you young blokes.' His big hands back on his hips. Stars and birds. Love on one set of fingers, smile on his face. Skin smeared off the knuckles. 'We can let this go now, can't we? We'll be on our way. I'm sorry about all the fuss.'

'Stupid old man. The last time I saw a head like that it had a hook in it.'

Ripples of laughter.

'Well,' Painter said, 'I got a head only a mother could love no doubt about it.'

Someone mimicked him in a high-pitched voice. 'No one would love that ugly fish head.'

They all laughed. Painter too, he was nodding. 'That'll do boys.' He cleared his throat. 'That'll do.'

'That'll do.' Again the insulting mimicry. 'Boys.'

More lifesavers had joined the group. The leader spoke. 'Who are you anyway? A stinkin' old dero by the look of you. Here on our beach. Old sailor are ya? Crim, just got out?'

Painter looked directly at him. 'A stinkin' old dero is it? That's me. A crim just got out.' He shrugged as if he was sick of trying. 'Yep and I was with your mother last night mate. Right here on the sand we did it. Almost to death we did it. And you know what? She was useless. Like a wet sack of wheat she was and smelled like an old dog left out in the rain for too long. I'd rather fuck a cricket bat than your mother. Probably thinking about you as I rooted her anyway son.'

Mr Kilpatrick would have turned away in disgust at such talk. Painter's chin lifted and he slipped his right shoulder for the left hook. Fists held at his waist. Nodding towards them. 'How do you like that? Boys? Come on now.'

Some of them seemed to pause, confused; someone said Jesus Christ while another two started laughing. Someone else said, 'No you weren't. She wasn't.'

'Step forward son,' Painter said to them all. 'Have a go. At me the ugly old bastard who fucked your mother. You got a sister? I bet you all know what's between her legs as well. A little wet slit in the dark under the blankets and do you dip your middle finger, smell it? Do you? You do, don't you?' Painter paused and looked at the eight or so lifesavers gathered around him. They just boys, never been hurt in their lives. God bless them they don't know what they are sayin' and I do. Children are easily frightened. He took a deep breath, coughed again and began rolling his fists in comic imitation of a fairground boxer. A carnival man.

'Be a man don't be afraid, look at me. A good horse never stumbles and a good mug never grumbles so give us the money boy and don't fuckin' sook about it like a fat girl with the smile and no ice-cream. My hand is open. Like your mother's legs. I am truly Mr Kilpatrick's disgrace. Punch as hard as you like. You cannot ever hurt me you young cunts.'

Lew had reached sandhills and tussock grass at the top of the beach. He knew what Painter would be saying. Tell them lies, boy, everyone believes what frightens them.

Fuck-off tauntings and feigned bewilderment; seeming friendliness and crude words as to take your breath away. Your mother's cunt, almost beautiful, the belief. Next, the humility amid the shocking humour; all the time looking for the weaknesses. Usually beat them before they start with the words if you can son, it's easier. Make them weak as they think.

Painter glanced to where he was, waited and nodded. Began to back away. Turned, walked and spun to face the following lifesavers. 'Wait a moment you. Don't get too close or I'll smack you down. By God I will and no jokin' now.'

Lew crossed the white shell-rock car park to the 1939 Ford pickup truck where they had parked it earlier. Got in, the door swinging open, and he was turning the key.

An empty clicking sound came from the engine.

'You're a bloody idiot son,' Painter yelled as he too reached the car park and waited at the verge. He was breathing hard. 'Look at us. Got no bearings here boy. We should have found a card game, something else, people we know. Who know us.'

'What?' Lew got out of the truck cab, slammed the door. He was carrying something as he walked to the front of the vehicle.

'Coming here,' Painter said. 'What's wrong?' He was speaking over his shoulder. Looking to his front and answering his own questions. 'Apart from you, that is, what's wrong. You young fool.'

'Won't start. Flat battery.'

'Jesus, son.'

Lew was trying to insert a crank handle into the truck's motor, his mouth still bleeding. Spat out spooling blood. Cheekbone swelling red. Left eye closing.

'What?'

Painter looked at the first of the lifesavers who had come up from the beach, pointed at him. They gathered and were standing at the edge of the sandy car park. The limestone bulk of the club pavilion behind them.

One of them called out, you better go all right you bastards, when the woman, the one Lew had been speaking to at the water's edge, pushed between them and walked to where he was trying to start the truck. She had a beach bag over her shoulder and a wide straw hat.

'Maureen?' A lifesaver called to her, stepped forward from the group. 'No, cut it out. Not with them, oh no. Maureen, come on?'

Lew was down on one knee, positioning the crank.

Painter was standing apart from them both, his hands on his

hips, glancing at Lew then at the ground. Towards the lifesavers.

Lew raised himself up and with all his strength pushed hard and down on the crank handle. The Ford caught and the motor began turning over.

'Can I come with you? Please.'

He stared at her and all he could think of was putting his fingers under her bathing costume, there at the top of her thighs. Lord, his thumb on her navel.

Painter heard and shook his head. 'No son.'

Lew said yes and she laughed, repeated Lew's yes and got into the truck. Said thank you. Threw the bag and hat in the space behind the drivers seat. The cab smelled of oil and hot metal. Cigarette smoke, raw wool and sweat.

Lew slid in behind the wheel. The navy blue stitched bench seat was sticky from the heat and she moved towards him to make room for where Painter would sit. Positioned herself so the gear stick was between her legs, the housing beneath her feet. He moved the gears through first to fourth and reverse while she opened her knees and thighs to allow him and stared straight ahead as he started to let the clutch out and looked back over his left shoulder. Touched him with her shoulder and elbow to say sorry. Lew smiled, no you don't have to.

Painter walked backwards and took three or four sidesteps towards the reversing truck. He jumped onto the running board, opened the door and swung in, shut the door as a limestone rock smashed against the windscreen. The glass cracked, didn't break, and another rock bounced off the bonnet. He coughed, stopped coughing and waited to cough again. Spat out the window and sat back in his seat.

'Good idea son,' he said, as they stopped reversing. Lew quickly changed gears and put his foot down on the accelerator pedal. 'Coming here.' The Ford jumped and juddered in a near-stall. White dust blowing around them.

Lew shook his head. 'You already said that.'

'Clutch,' Painter said. Lew slammed his foot on the clutch, corrected the stall and managed to get the car moving from the beach. Changed gears as Painter said, 'Change bloody gears go on. That's it.'

They drove away fishtailing along the sandy track towards Fremantle. Norfolk pines and white sand dunes covered in moving marram grass. A blacktop macadamised road crumbling at the edges and the blue sky and the Indian Ocean away to their right for as far as they could see. Fifteen or so merchant ships in Gage Roads.

'Mr Jesus where are you now?' Painter said.

'What was that?'

'I wasn't talkin' to you. What's the name of this place again?'

'Cottesloe,' Lew said. Looked at the woman.

She nodded. 'Cottesloe Beach.'

'Slow down.' Painter leaned forward and looked at him.

Lew ignored Painter and turned again to the woman. 'Can I ask you your name?'

'Maureen,' she said. 'Maureen O'Reilly.'

He felt her leg move against him.

Painter had an unlit smoke in his mouth, his arms folded. He shook his head and looked out at the passing Norfolk pines. Said something to himself, shook his head once again.

The muscle in Lew's jaw clenched again. He nodded.

'And no bloody lifesavers again neither.'
She said, 'I can swim Lew. I can teach you.'
'What?'
'I'm sorry,' she said.
'No, it's all right.'

There were engine parts and tools scattered about the floor. A tall stack of tyres; gearboxes in pieces. Wheel rims and a back axle. The light came through lopsided venetian blinds. A west window with faded Caltex and Chevrolet stickers stuck to it. Ford and Chrysler. A 1940 Shell calendar above a desk and an old chair pushed back as if someone had just got up from it.

Her eyes were closed and she had taken off her shoes. The oil-black concrete beneath her bare feet. 'You should not be here,' she said, 'I should not, I am thirty-seven.' Looked at him as if this was enough.

'Maureen.'

She stood on one foot to remove her underwear. Whispered, 'My, Mr Peter O'Reilly.'

'My name is Lewis.'

'No...not you.' She placed a flat hand against his chest and smiled into his face. 'Not you baby.'

'Who?'

'No one.' Her hands were undoing his belt, the buttons of his trousers and he could smell her damp hair as she looked down, said, 'You,' and then, as if beside herself, 'just fuck me.' Her legs coming around his legs.

It was another two days before he knocked on the door of the house in front of the Motor Garage in East Fremantle. P J & M M O'Reilly Mechanical Repairs and Services East Fremantle Motors Ltd. A big blue sign.

She opened the front door and glanced behind. Stepped out, holding the door almost closed with one hand.

'Hello Maureen,' he said.

'It's you,' she said, and raised her wrist to her mouth. A sea wind moved her cotton print dress away from her and she smoothed her brown hair back behind her ear. A straight mouth as she smiled with her lips closed.

He could hear a baby crying and the voice of an older woman from behind her, inside the house. 'Who is it Maureeney love?'

'No one Mum.' She looked back at him. 'Sorry, but I have forgotten your name.'

'Lewis,' he said. 'I told you the other day.'

'Lewis.' Maureen studied him for a few moments. 'Are you all right?'

'I'm all right. Been thinking about you though. Can't stop. All the time it seems.'

'I know.'

He was quiet, unable to understand what she was telling him. And then he did and turned away as his mouth was to break apart and walked down the steps to where he had parked the Ford.

'Love,' she called out as he reached the bottom of the steps and was opening the gate.

He didn't look back or think for a moment that she did what she said. Most likely just a name, a habit she had. Even something in the workshop. A lot of women called men love when they said goodbye. Or even hello. That was all right too. Do you want a cup of tea love? They said that.

Lew spent the remainder of the morning finding his way back to their free camp on the Djarlgarra. He drove along the Canning Road until he reached the Albany Highway. Left off onto a gravel road that led to the wild disused land along the riverbanks. He passed between swamp banksias and paperbarks.

Wetland birds rising from the reeds. The heavy lifting of pelican through the cumbungi and bulrush. Smelled the clean air coming from the river water and drove through casuarinas. He stopped the truck once to relieve himself and then he drove on. After a quarter of a mile he came to the old barge horse path near Mason's Landing. It was overgrown with wild oats and prickly dryandra.

He bumped through the bushes scraping along the sides of the truck. Followed the sunken dirt track until he reached their camp. Stopped in a small clearing and switched off the engine. Cicadas were loud in the sunshine and two or three ringneck parrots flew away through the trees, calling out their number;

being cheeky bastards Painter would say, listen to them, the twenty-eights.

Lew got out of the truck, slammed the door, said fuck it and began to pack up his tent. He rolled his swag and put canvas bags in the back of the truck. Threw the tent poles, clattering, into the tray. Raised one hand in greeting towards Painter who was standing next to the campfire.

'Didn't expect to see you till tomorrow son. Maybe day after,' he said, holding a fork. 'Looks like our time in the big smoke's over, is it?'

'I'm off. You coming?' Lew, using his elbow and palm as a template, began rolling up a length of rope. 'I heard there's a bit of fencing work down south round Dardanup.'

Painter scratched his arm with the fork. 'Dunno bout that but we still got that charcoal contract northeast of Boddington. Should start it next few days.'

'Well fuck that,' Lew said.

'Yep.' Painter scratched his shoulder with the fork again. 'Then, next month, north and further out, four days shearing on the Drysdales' place. You want to fuck that as well?'

Lew finished coiling the rope and looped two holding hitches into the middle of the roll. Threw it next to the swag and tent poles in the back of the truck. Opened the truck door and stood holding it open. One boot on the running board. 'Think you're funny don't you? Sayin' that? You been drinkin'?'

'No.'

'Good. What about that fencing job?'

'By the time we finish the charcoal, be time to start shearing at Drysdale's anyway. I just told you.'

Lew hadn't let go of the truck door. 'I been thinking about doing some prospecting.'

Painter walked over to the truck, reached in, pulled Lew's swag out and dropped it beside the back wheels. 'You have?'

'Yep.' Lew, watching what Painter was doing, continued to speak. 'There's an old bloke out there, past the Drysdales'. I heard about him. He's got some gear we can use. Way out by that abandoned town, Thompson's Find, something like that.'

'That's what they call wajil country son.' Painter shook his head as he returned to the campfire. 'Mulga, jam tree. Useless bloody land. Good for bugger all and no one in their right mind goes there.' He placed a few more small pieces of wood on the flames. 'I know about that old bloke, scratches a living fetching sandalwood. Fossicks for gold. Old Dingo Smith, some of the farmers call him. There is no gold, but he needs a reason to make butter. A top dog man, shooter. That's how he gets by for the most part. Taking dingo, there's the name.'

'I thought he was a gold miner.'

'No. He is a dingo hunter, gold was an excuse, why else would he stay there? He loves being alone and he loves killing dogs. Some say he doesn't know his arse from his elbow, drinking and barking at the moon, dances with one of them goats he keeps. Calls her Eunice, everyone knows. But as far as cleaning the place up? Best there ever was, some say. Wanted to be a miner, no good at it.'

'Eunice? Dances with a goat? Cut it out.'

'Well.' Painter looked directly at him. 'I dunno. But when it comes to gold and goats and women a lot of blokes go a bit silly in the head.'

Lew nodded at the swag on the ground. 'Get fucked.'

Painter's laughter as he turned away. His mouth open, imitating Lew, repeating what he said, 'Get fucked.' Scratched the side of his face, still with the fork, and touched what was left of his nose. 'Young Mr McCleod. You growin' up son. Yes you are.' Laughed for a while longer.

A small camp oven hanging from a hook and chain on an iron tripod. The lid just tilted up on the rim to let the steam escape. On a nearby fold-out table, two enamel plates. Flour in one and a blood-stained white cloth covering something on the other. Flies circling. Painter waved his hands over the plates. 'I am cooking this underground mutton here. You are welcome to it son.'

Lew had closed the truck door and sat on the running board, put one ankle on his knee. Took off his right boot and sock. Crossed his leg, removed his other boot and sock, put both feet on the ground and rubbed them into the sand. 'How many you get?'

Painter, kneeling next to the fire, held up three fingers as he took a flat black-iron pan and placed it into the fire on an iron cob. Spooned in some mutton dripping and watched as it began to melt and slide. Lifted the muslin cloth and picked up a back quarter of the rabbit, laid it in the flour and then into the hot pan. He did this with three more pieces and waved his hand above the cooking. The sound of the rabbit frying in the pan. A small wind blew across the river. The riverside bulrushes and cumbungi rustling.

'Smells good mate.'

Painter took a black kettle from the side of the fire and dropped in a handful of loose tea. Wiped the fork on his pants and used it to stir the tea-leaves into the hot water. Put the kettle to one side in the sand. Nodded towards the swag. 'Might as well unroll that, son. Go on now.'

Lew had his elbows on his knees. He nodded and watched his bare feet in the dust.

Maureen said that her husband Peter had been in Libya with the Australian 6th Division. He was a hero, she said, and a corporal. He's still there, she said, buttoning her dress, leaning down to put on a shoe. Two fingers in the heel, hopped on one foot and held Peter's old workbench for balance. The Shell Oil calendar on the wall.

I married quite young, she said. A row of spanners above the bench. She couldn't bring herself to take down the sign over the garage. He had loved the East Fremantle Football Club, she said. The mighty Sharks. His brother was one of those lifesavers at Cottesloe. Didn't know it was your brother-in-law, he told her. That's why they were so bloody angry at us. It was you Maureen. It was you, I thought it was us being there. That too, she said.

'She knew what to do, Painter,' he said to his feet.

Painter cleared his throat and used the fork to turn the frying rabbit. He nodded and turned the other three pieces. 'That's good.'

'What's good?'

'That's good son cause you don't.'

'What do you mean?'

'Everybody remembers their first, mate.' He had placed the fried rabbit onto a plate. 'Most of us clumsy as a fool.' He lifted the lid from the camp oven. 'All back legs and tail.'

Painter let the rabbit pieces slide into the camp oven. Used the fork to move them. 'And make a flat-out bloody idiot of ourselves,' he said. 'The flour will thicken it. Quite a few even run away. Easier, see.'

'What you think?'

'About what?'

'About her? Me?'

'She's heartbroken son. Nothing to do with you. Can't help it.' Painter took a rabbit shoulder and laid one side in the flour. Turned it over, white side up.

'Heartbroken?' Lew rubbed his hand over his face. 'She didn't want to see me again, forgot my name,' he said. 'Told me she was thirty-seven and called me Peter O'Reilly. Jesus, I think he was her dead husband, then she said I was not him, Jesus fuckin' wept. Then did it with me…I can't think of anything else but her…and her legs around me and what she said with her dress up around her waist. Jesus.'

'Don't say Jesus like that so much.' Painter touched a swollen lump on his head where a lifesaver had hit him. Thumb pressing above his eyebrow. 'You ever see a woman having a baby? Giving birth?'

'What?'

'Fucking mess. All over the bloody bed and floor, shit everywhere. Like an animal they are.' Painter stood up and poured tea into two enamel mugs. Put one next to Lew's foot and concentrated on flouring the next few pieces of rabbit. Laid them in the shimmering fat of the pan.

'There was a baby crying,' Lew said. 'Couldn't be her dead husband's anyway. Too young.'

Painter nodded and began to roll another smoke. He put the unlit cigarette in his mouth and prodded the browning rabbit with the fork. Spooned in more mutton fat, turned the pieces and lit his smoke.

He was about nine feet in the air, leaning over the top of a black conical charcoal kiln and smoothing wet clay on the widening cracks. It had been burning for five days and the charcoal would be ready to uncover, cool and stack tomorrow.

Painter had positioned upright jarrah poles, a yard long and about six inches in diameter, two feet apart, around the base, secured smaller cross branches on top of the poles and was standing on these branches as he worked. Thin white smoke easing out above him. His hands, arms and chest splattered with red clay. A beaten-up Traveller hat on his head and now he was wearing sandshoes on his feet. Balancing on the cross branches, he looked down at Lew. 'This burn's finished pretty much, take a day to cool no worries son. Sixteen hundredweight I reckon.'

Lew held a tall Henry Dilston and Sons crosscut log saw and was sitting on one of two cross-pole sawhorses. Four cords of jarrah and marri stacked behind him.

They had laid out corrugated-iron sheets to deter termites.

This would be ready for the next burning. More sheets of corrugated iron roofed the cords. They had weighed down the iron with logs and stones. Behind Lew, a makeshift workbench with two attached vices. Three Kelly axes lying flat on the benchtop alongside a stand of wooden-handled flat, fine and half-round files.

The bush surrounding them was olive green, grey and black. Straight, brilliant white trees and blackened bloodwoods. Smoke bush and granite heather. Prickly Moses. Painter had rigged a sharpening stone with a foot treadle and an upturned kerosene tin as a seat. Two canvas tents and an open fireplace with the iron tripod holding a black billy tin. Smoke was drifting from the campfire. Another axe driven into a tree stump. An American.

The truck was parked at the edge of the clearing. Clothes, trousers and shirts laid out on the bonnet and roof to dry. A track through umbrella wattle bushes led away from the clearing towards a wider, two-wheel dirt road running parallel to a rail line. Painter climbed down from the charcoal kiln and slapped his hands together.

'Abdul and Wahid be here to pick up the charcoal day after tomorrow.' He took out a round blue tin of Capstan tobacco, opened it, removed a cigarette paper, stuck it to his bottom lip and began to roll the tobacco in his palm.

'Abdul. Wahid? They got camels?'

Painter shrugged. 'Afghans. Probably got camels.'

They sat on a log, drank black tea and ate damper spread with golden syrup. Lew watched one of his bare feet as it made a furrow in the sand.

'Still like your bare feet in the ground son,' Painter said.

'Never had shoes in my life till I started work in the sheds. You teased me, remember?'

Painter took the white paper off his lip, placed the tobacco into the paper. His fingers and thumbs working on the smoke. Nodded. 'Barefoot kid turned up for work in the shearing gang. That contractor dropped you off. You were what?...Seven? Twelve?' Painter cleared his throat.

'Eleven. I was eleven.'

The next day, two Afghans from Coolgardie arrived and asked how're ya goin'? Trans Australian Transport 1933. Boulder. Ph 613 written on the door of their green Chevrolet.

Painter whispering to Lew, urging him to ask Abdul where his camels were. They were a long way from home after all. 'Go on,' he said, 'they'll appreciate it.'

'Where are all your camels Abdul?' Lew was completely black from the charcoal dust. His white eyes and teeth.

Abdul glaring at him as he tied a tarpaulin over the charcoal. Shook his head. 'You some sort of a smart-arse mate?'

Painter walking into the mallee, bending over and holding a branch; laughing so hard he began to cry.

That night the fire had burnt down to a red glow and Lew was leaning forward, reading a magazine by the light of a Coleman lamp. He was sitting on a canvas camp chair in front of the fly of his tent. His finger followed the words and his mouth moved occasionally as he read. The lamp was between his feet and trunks of large salmon gums were shining behind him.

They had washed with a bushman's shower rigged up with a

Baird hand pump and tin bath. Salvaged water from the railway depot. Sunlight soap. The water was black when they threw it out.

Painter was seated at a fold-out card table and in front of him, spread out on a towel, were cutters and combs, a shearing handpiece. He was examining the gear by the light of the fire and another kerosene lamp on the table. An unlit cigarette dangling from his mouth. 'What you reading son?'

Lew turned the magazine towards him. 'There's a story in it. I read it before anyway.' Pointed his finger at the title. 'Him.'

'Who is it? Banjo?' Painter peered at the yellowed pages. 'How many times you read that?'

'Henry. A few times mate. My mother read it to me.'

'I heard about that poor old bastard Henry. Heard he sung out at the end that he should have been a woman. What you reckon? Cried for it.'

'He was gone mad and pissed to bits half the time mate. He could have said he should have been a fuckin' bird of paradise.'

Painter nodded. Threaded some cutters onto a piece of number-eight wire bent into a long fish-hook shape. 'A bird of paradise?' He waited, glanced at Lew. 'Not a woman, then?' He placed the cutters into a leather bag and began holding each of the combs up to the lamplight.

Lew ignored Painter's taunt. 'Our mother hated this story. Flat out looking after us kids and it was every day, mate, every day. Trying to follow Dad all over too. One day it all got too hard and we just stopped. That wheatbelt rail town. Blackwood Junction, we stayed on for a bit there.'

'I know Blackwood Junction. Never met your father but.'

'He just left. Nothing. Took off like a dog shot up the arse. Methodists helped us out. Mum'd say, when it was cold she'd say it was cold as charity. But y'know. The women would smile and say Jesus loves you. Give us a lot of food and never asked for anything back.'

Painter was running his forefinger along the comb teeth. Frowning in the lamplight. 'They all right. The Methodists.' He was squinting as he spoke. 'I think I need glasses. She did all right too. Your mum. You always reading whenever you can, seen you read the labels of tins.'

'Yeah. But not all her dogs barking sometimes, y'know?' Lew pointed his finger at his ear and made a circling motion. 'After Dad.'

Painter wrapped his combs in a length of leather and carefully folded them away in the bag. 'Some things don't need to be said son. No need.' He placed a shearing handpiece on the table. It was wrapped in oily rags. 'The old lizard,' he said.

'She had a copy of *Robbery Under Arms*,' Lew said, 'and Ginger Mick. Jist to intrajuice me cobber, a rorty boy a naughty boy. But Henry, too sad, she said. Too real.' Lew held the magazine up, shook it. 'I told her it's just a story Mum. Not what is. Oh yes it is, she said, that's the point isn't it? He must have known.'

Painter picked up the handpiece and turned it over in his hands, put a thumb into the turning gear and rotated the moving parts. 'You mean the bird of paradise?' Winked at him. 'Sad lookin' bastard, Henry, did you ever cop a picture of him? Maudlin cunt of a thing he was.'

'Yep, I have.' Lew laughed.

30

Painter smoked. Nodded and made a noise of agreement, sniffed. 'I never knew me mother, y'know. I'm what they call a foundling orphan out of Kalgoorlie me.'

'Kalgoorlie?' In ten years, Lew had never heard Painter speak of his past. 'Your mum?'

'To be honest she probably a whore, working on Hay Street, y'know? Hawking the fork and thinking about buying corrugated iron.' Painter winked, his mouth thin. 'Ever hear the way their head bangs on the wall when you fuck them?'

Lew looked at him. 'No. Sorry mate.'

Painter waited, shifted his weight in the chair, the canvas creaked. 'Don't ever fuckin' sorry me son.' Cleared his throat. 'I'll knock you down. You hear?' Relit the cigarette which had gone out in his mouth. 'You know what a Fitzroy cocktail is?'

'No. No I don't.'

'You drink it. Cheap, see. Methylated spirits mixed with Brasso. Strain the metho through a loaf of bread. Mix the Brasso in, it turns a cloudy colour. Give you an off balance no worries son.'

'Yeah?'

'Good company and doesn't ask questions. Tastes like wet bread and fuckin' door handles.'

'Jesus.'

Painter gave a short laugh. 'I was inside. That's where I learned that.'

Lew stared at him. 'You been drinking haven't you?

'No I haven't been drinkin'.'

'You were in prison?'

'I was inside for a while. Just don't ask me why. All right?'

'Righto.' Lew couldn't look at him, nodded as the old man continued.

'I got out and I was sent to the sheds. They needed what they called manpower on the land see; most of the men away at the war. I didn't go. Then I was caught and I went. Almost forty years now gone it's been. Nineteen fifteen, sixteen. Our vast land they called it.'

'Righto.'

Painter suddenly growled and held up an impatient hand, moving it back and forth almost as if he was trying to stop the words of an unwelcome visitor. 'I knew this other bloke was all alone in the cell next door. True as I sit here. He existed. No hope and him knocked about. I couldn't hear him breathing, see.'

'Who mate?' Lew asked. He had heard fragments of this before, mostly when the old man was drunk. Once, when it was very bad, he had wept.

A minute passed. 'It was me I was talkin' to, son. Took a while to work it out. I was slapping my hands on the limestone and singin' out to the other bloke. All the old lags thought the same. Whisperin' out of the sides of their mouths, they were mostly gone mad and plain stupid with the scars all over them, no doubt about it. But, when you start talkin' to yourself, they said, you think you are someone else. Ready for Jesus or sideways son, y'know? I got Jesus.'

Painter stopped talking, looked away, embarrassed, realising he had been speaking too much. 'Fuck.' He stood up and made his way to his tent.

'Night son.'

'Night.'

'I dunno what.' Painter turned and knelt to disappear into his tent. 'Doesn't matter.'

Later that night, Lew dreamed of his mother. He was sitting on the edge of a veranda listening to laughter coming from a public bar. His feet in the dust and his mother, dancing inside with bare feet. She would never do this, something was wrong. Her shoes in the street, straps undone.

He woke. Painter was somewhere nearby, snoring softly. Occasionally he would mumble something. The dream was as clear as memory. It was as if he could hear his mother's voice yet. Couldn't see her face, not much of it anyway. Remembered mostly her hands and the feeling of becoming weightless when she lifted him up onto her hip and kissed him on the mouth. Everybody had bare feet then. Her hands smelling of wet potatoes and flour.

A shearing contractor who knew his father had asked his mother if the oldest boy needed a job. Price of wool going through the roof, see, be a pound a pound before long and you with all those kiddies missus. Smart thing to do, with a wink and a finger tapping the side of his nose. Smart thing for you all. A lot of the men not right still or away over there. The country will be riding on the sheep's back after the war, the newspapers reckon. A boom.

'On the sheep's back,' she said. 'I have heard that. That'll be good, won't it?'

The contractor left a letter from their father, a brown paper parcel and a white carton of tailor-made American cigarettes with a big red circle on them. Lucky Strike Toasted plain cut.

Lew would remember his mother holding the carton as she hugged him and told him to do his best. The crinkly sound of the cellophane. The other kids around them like chooks as he tried to say goodbye Mum. She was holding the carton of cigarettes to her chest. No tears in her eyes this time, nodding and trying to smile. Then, breathless and coughing, with her wrist up to her mouth.

The contractor dropped him off at the shed and nodded to the drunk Painter. He seemed to be always drunk in those days. He was the Ringer, the fearful head shearer. Lew could not look at him and stared instead at his feet. The contractor seemed nervous and left quickly, speaking over his shoulder. 'Show him the ropes will you Painter? He might be all right if he's anything like his father.'

'Son,' Painter ignored the contractor and spoke to him, 'do you know a shearer is just a rousie with his brains knocked out?'

Looked to where Lew was looking at his feet and shaking his head.

'What's your name boy?'

'Lew.'

'Lew who?'

'Lew McCleod.'

'Well now Mr McCleod. You got nothing on your feet son?'

'No mister.'

'Come on then.'

Painter took him to the end of the shed near the Ferrier wool press. 'Put your foot on there. I'll make you some dancing shoes.'

Painter doubled a jute sacking fadge top and placed it on the floor. Lew stepped on it and Painter cut around the outline of his foot with a pair of crutching hand shears. He left a wide overlap at the front, sewed up the heel, tied it off and gathered the sacking around Lew's toes. Then, using a blanket stitch, sewed it all together. Pulled it tight. 'How's that feel son?'

'Good thank you Mr Painter.'

'Well you make the other one. I haven't got time to fuck around with you.' Winked at Lew. 'Boy turning up to work barefoot, like a Kalgoorlie orphan. You ever had shoes boy? Shoes for church?'

Lew, silent.

'Jesus son.'

'I'm sorry,' he said.

'Don't fuckin' sorry me mate. I'll knock you down.' Painter winked and waited, studying Lew's face before he spoke again. 'Don't worry, you can't help it son. I don't go neither. Mob of cunts. Don't reckon the other bloke would recognise a single one.'

First man that ever called him mate or son or Mr McCleod and he didn't have a clue what the tattooed drunk was saying most of the time. He made the other woolshed dancing shoe but it wasn't as good as Painter's.

It wasn't long after that Painter began to teach him to shear. 'Don't try,' he would say. 'Let the handpiece do the work. The old lizard. Feel it become the end of your arm, your natural hand. Soon enough you will be a gun. A two hundred a day man. Ringer in the shed like me. Now the best thing you can do is shut your mouth and do what you are told.'

He learned to curse. To use foul and profane language as a matter of course. To lie to tell the truth and distrust the truth as a lie. He learned to survive. To fight. Discovered an affinity with mechanical things. The workings of motors. He was taught to use a rifle and a shotgun by an unmarried station owner who asked if he would stay on. He said he needed a mate and could teach him to shoot kangaroos, fox and dingo.

The smell of beer and whisky on Painter. The stink of his old sweat. Tobacco. And how he would say, over and over, let the handpiece do the work boy. Don't think about your hand or yourself and the pain you feel, just let it know by itself. And bloody keep going young Mr McCleod. Never give up boy.

In the mornings Painter would vomit in the catching pen before he started shearing. Shaking. Got the ta-tas, he would say. Then he would start drinking from the bottle wrapped in wet newspaper and rubber bands. Sometimes he would shit himself. Blood too, but he never stopped working.

By the time Lew was sixteen he could shear one hundred and eighty sheep a day and Painter had become extraordinarily proud of him. Almost always called him son. And sometimes Mr McCleod. By the time he was twenty-one, two hundred and fifty a day. He never saw his mother again.

They drove through the night. East into a rising moon. A faint white light under the speedometer in the dashboard. Occasionally the cab would flare bright around Painter's head as he lit another cigarette. Otherwise it was the moonlight and the reach of the truck headlights through the country as they travelled into the marginal wheat and sheep lands.

Painter leaned forward, turned his head and looked up at the black sky above them. The huge arch and swirl of stars across the night. 'Look at that,' he said. 'A blackfella once told me they up there…the stars?…Babies hiding in an old woman's hair.'

Lew stared straight ahead at the narrow road and nodded. Said, 'Hold on a bit.' Slowed down as they ran into a badly potholed stretch of road. The truck juddering as they passed over the corrugations.

When they had cleared it Lew glanced out at the sky. 'Babies hiding in an old woman's hair you say.'

'That's the story.'

'You could see why, if you thought about it like that, couldn't you?'

'You could.'

'Henry would see it Painter. He would.'

'You think he would? Bit of a no-hoper, old Henry in his day.'

'That's what the lifesavers at Cottesloe called us mate. No-hopers.'

And Painter was laughing. 'Well they got that right then son. Didn't they?'

Ten minutes later they stopped. Lew refilled the petrol tank from a forty-four-gallon drum secured on the tray behind the cab, then walked a little way off the track to urinate. He heard Painter get out of the truck and he too walked to the side of the road to piss. When he finished he buttoned his moleskins.

Painter had put his hands on his hips and was again staring at the brilliance of the night sky. It was such as to be impossible to ignore, spangled, silent and violent for as far as they could see. Just the sound of the wind in the night. 'You can see the Seven Sisters Lew.' He pointed at the Pleiades constellation. 'And the Flat-out Emu.'

Lew walked to the truck and looked back at Painter in the glow of the stars and the rising full moon. 'Come on mate, we better keep moving.'

'Would you look at it?' Painter had his head back and was staring at the sky. 'It doesn't go away. No matter what.'

'You all right?'

Painter didn't reply for a while.

'Yeah. It's just the sky. Won't leave me alone tonight it seems.'

'Come on.'

They got into the truck and closed the doors. Lew turned the starter motor, the engine fired, began to run. They sat and listened to the running of the Ford, a rumbling low steadiness. Painter nodded and cleared his throat. 'You heard about the man in the moon son?'

'Always looked a bit like a rabbit to me.'

Painter laughed and Lew glanced at him and grinned as they drove off.

The old man kept staring at the moon. It had grown larger and was blue-white and in places shaded, covered in scars. The craters formed by the impacts of meteorites. The still mountains, and dark seas of sand.

'I heard more of them blackfella stories, one of a sun woman,' Painter said. 'Makes the moon run away, she does. The night go. Sister sun he called her. No more blackfellas out here but. Used to be a swag of them, camped out around Daybreak Springs used to be Winjilla.'

'What?' Lew raising his voice over the noise of the engine. 'Did you say sun woman at Daybreak Springs?'

'That's part of Drysdale Downs station. Old man Drysdale took it when he come up from Kalgoorlie. Hundreds of thousands of acres given away mate, you just had to show proof of improvement. Old Jungle Forrest did that to open up the show for farming. Before the Boer War.'

The moonlight on the bonnet and both halves of the cracked windscreen glinting.

'And no blackfellas workin' on the Drysdale station now, you say?' Lew asked. 'Some of the best shearers but. Top blokes, women rousies too, they like shadows laughing in a woolshed. Never seen better.'

'No blackfellas on Drysdale Downs. Never will be. All gone.'

'Why's that mate?'

'Old man Drysdale and Dingo Smith persuaded them to move down south to round Boddington just after the first war,' Painter said. 'Never come back.'

'Persuaded.' Lew glanced over at him in the light coming from the dashboard. 'How'd they do that?'

Painter, in shadow, held up his hand, cocked his wrist and pulled a trigger with his index finger.

They were quiet, listening to the sounds of the truck travelling on the dirt road. The gravel whipping under the mudguards. The headlight beams searching out in front of them.

'You believe that?'

Painter wound down the window, cleared his throat and spat into the passing night.

'I do believe that.'

Wound up the window and after a few minutes he turned his shoulder into the corner of the cab and tilted his hat over his eyes. A rolled towel under his head. Folded his arms. 'I might have a sleep. You right?'

'Yeah I'm good. You sleep.'

Soon his breathing lengthened and he began to snore. Every now and again he would unfold his arms and touch what was left of his nose with his thumb. Open and close his mouth, fold and refold his arms. Murmur something and cough with his eyes shut.

Lew watched the road and the headlights playing over it and the scrub and smoke bush. White wandoo gums in groups alongside the roadside. Ghosts, journey watchers. He thought of Maureen at the beach, scooping up handfuls of sea water, placing her flat hands on his chest, and then he did not want to think of her and he drove and looked out at the passing land in the moonlight. Hummed a tune he had heard on the radio, Streets of Laredo.

A great thump hit the side of the truck and he saw two grey kangaroos bound through the headlights. Another thump and three more crossed ahead of them. The perfect curve of their backs, tails in counterbalance. He braked but it was too late. The truck collided with another in mid-flight. It came up onto the bonnet, smashing into the already cracked windscreen, shattering it. Disappeared.

They came to a sliding stop, sideways on the road. A single headlight shining away into the scrub through the dust.

'What? Hold on. Hold on.' Painter shouting as he was thrown awake. Broken glass falling over him.

'Mob of roos mate.' Lew was looking back. He put the truck into neutral and pulled on the handbrake. 'We hit one.' He was opening the door. 'Maybe two heads there.'

Painter was moving also. Quick for an old man. Lew heard the opening and closing of his door, the crunch of broken glass. He was standing at the front mudguard. Running his hand over the bumper for damage. One of the headlights out.

He disappeared and after a minute came walking back along the road, brushing at his clothing with one hand, stopped and stepped into the light of the remaining headlight. A haze of moving dust. He was holding something; lifted it.

'She's here son'. Held a baby kangaroo up by its back legs. 'And this is your second head mate. It's a little joey all right. Noongar call them nyarnyee.'

The baby swayed and tried to kick out. Jerking to be away. Painter held it away from his body, waited for a minute and then swung it up and in a circle to smash its head against a roadside gum. 'Yeah, nyarnyee. Bye bye baby bye bye.'

'No,' Lew called out. 'Don't.'

Painter aborted the killing swing, lifting his arm so the head of the joey missed the tree trunk by a few inches. He rested it on the ground and it click-hissed and mewed, feet jerking, desperate to run. 'What?' He stared at Lew. 'It's kinder.' He put a foot on the joey's head to keep it still.

'Hold on a sec.' Lew walked to the truck and came back with an old grey blanket and a length of rope. He took the joey and bound it tightly in the blanket. Tied the rope around the bottom and under its front paws. Its head stuck out of the bundle. It shook its head and blinked. Little ears flapping, turning, moving independently of each other as to make you laugh.

'What are you doing?' Painter asked.

Lew ignored him and spoke to the joey. 'You bloody thing,' he said. 'You beautiful little bloody thing you.' He laughed. Its tiny nostrils opening and closing at him. Ears flicking back and forth. 'Mum's gone, dead, sorry little one.'

The joey blinked again and struggled in the blanket. The

high-pitched clicking noise coming from its throat. Lew put one hand over its eyes and pulled the blanket across its head. Held it as you would a child and it stilled immediately.

'I don't know,' Painter said and walked off into the scrub.

After a few minutes Lew saw him emerge. He was dragging the body of the mother by the tail. He pulled it into the road where it was lit by the truck's headlight, dropped the carcass and walked to the back of the truck and returned with a butchers knife.

'I'll take her tail,' he said, 'she's fresh enough.' Bent over the carcass and used the knife to cut the tail from her body. 'For soup. Beautiful. Look.'

He held up the dripping tail.

'Jesus,' Lew said and turned away.

'What?'

The sun woman's fire spread across the sky as the moon fled and the red light came down and over them all. A great flock of pink and grey galahs flew above the road and Lew watched as the light rose and for as far as he could see, the earth turned pale blue and mauve in the smoky pink of early morning. The sunlight coming over the horizon and into his eyes. It blinded him as he sat up in the truck. The sun rising quickly now. Painter also woke.

The dingo bitch rose from her belly, squatted and pissed. Her tail flexed twice and then she turned and smelled the place she had pissed. Circled and flattened against the earth, all the time watching the carcass of the grey doe bloating in the heat. Suns reflected from shards of broken glass. The meeyal truck on the side of the road. The mob she had been chasing that night long gone, the desperate mother hit by the truck, the yonga, her tail cut from her, on the roadside.

She watched in the sunlight of the morning as the men got out of the truck and they too pissed. They were downwind of her and she lifted her nose to their kidney smell, the water flattening in the wind. How far it fell from their bodies. Young man old man. They got back in the truck and drove away.

She saw the truck disappear in the dust and lay motionless. Her nose quivering, testing the air, her ears pricked. There was only the ground and sky noise when the sound of the truck faded. The dust settled and the east wind came. Rivers of scent.

The man road and the stinking vehicles. Blown dust crossed the road.

She stood, her mouth opened and she panted. Flies buzzed above the doe and she could see ants in the black seeping blood.

The old man had taken her tail and her young, had dragged the body off to one side. She crossed to where the two men had been that morning and smelled where they had urinated and then she squatted and also pissed over their markings. Her tail curved as she checked the spoor of her leaving. Defecated and repeated the circling. Scratched sand behind her to cover the dropping. The smell of the old man and young man were different.

The dingo studied the dead kangaroo and the surrounds for a while longer.

Her eyes drooped and she licked at her shoulder, a healing wound the black dingo had made with his slashing teeth as he mated with her. The black dog was strong, crossed with one of the big run-off cattle-station dogs.

They had become welded when he covered her and finished, knotted with his swollen glands locked inside. She had yelped, turned and bitten at him, opening his ear. His dominance reasserted itself and he stood snarling over her with strong, straight legs. She obeyed with look-away eyes and became still for him as they waited. And then he slipped out, and was gone. Head down running west and never looking back at her. Ten minutes later her nose was following where his feet and saliva had touched the rocks and sand. The rapture of what would become a pack, twelve or so dingos, running in and beside her.

She felt a twist of hunger for six and stood. Approached the yonga carcass from a side angle, bent her head under where the tail had been taken and began tearing at the flesh. Soon she had exposed the intestines. Swallowed a mouthful of gut fat. The doe's soft liver, pulpy in her mouth. The dingo bitch gulped the liver and choked. Vomited up the black mess and began to eat it again.

It was mid-morning when they turned off the Great Eastern Highway, rattled across the rails of a cattleguard and onto the red mile that led to Drysdale Downs homestead. They passed a five-wire fence. Iron star pickets and two top barbed, wool stuck in the barbs. The dried bodies of several wild dogs had been wired with ancient spines and leg shapes outstretched on the fence. Paddocks of dried mitchell and failed flinders grasses, yellow grass and smoke bush out to a series of hollows and rises away to the horizon. Beyond there the wheat fields.

Three pink and grey galahs flew off the fence at their approach.

'Drysdale Downs,' Lew said. His voice croaking from the dry silence. 'How many they got?'

'Not as many as they used to,' Painter said. 'About twelve hundred I believe. Three maybe four days for us.' He coughed. 'Used to run over ten thousand head but they gone mostly to wheat now anyway. Should be the other way around. Dunno if they got shed hands coming even, it's all a bit of a doubt mate.'

'No blackfellas you say? None?'

'Not now, not ever. I told you. They will never lay a foot here. None bloody left.'

A Comet windmill in the near paddock. Tall and rusted tubes welded into a thin quadruped structure with a working platform bolted below the circle of blades. Long curved metal flukes. A bent pipe running from the top of the bore to the holding tank. Two stone drinking troughs north south.

'Something else I should tell you,' Painter said. 'Pull up here for a bit.'

Lew stopped the truck at the side of the track. Stones crunched beneath the tyres. He looked over at Painter.

'The boss, John Drysdale, lost his wife a few years ago. Had their share of troubles on the place, her was just the latest.'

Lew with both wrists on the steering wheel, leaned forward, watching. 'Lost?'

'Cancer. Yep. Jack the dancer, y'know.' Painter stared out the side window. 'Took it hard I heard. Like a dry stick in the wind these days.'

'By himself now?'

'No, a daughter, she was at boarding school in Perth. She come home I believe. Clara, her name. Thought I would let you know to tread a little careful, y'know, ducks on the pond. Less said the better.'

Lew nodded. 'I'll keep it in mind.' He eased the clutch pedal out.

'Have you seen that?' Painter nodded out the window as they drove. An ancient red harrow rusting at the edge of the paddock. Its metal seat, buttock-shaped and perforated, high above the metal spines. Rusted trace chains. Large spoke wheels. Abandoned but kept, grown around like a wound. Long wheat grass through it.

'Yeah mate. An old harrow.'

They drove up to a shearing shed raised up on wandoo stumps. Pulled the truck to a stop and waited for the dust to settle. They got out of the truck, closed the doors and stretched. Hands braced above kidneys.

A blue heeler cattle dog ran from the yards and began barking. John Drysdale walked from the woolshed, holding up one hand to block the sun and looking at them. A tall, lean man, dressed in a faded green shirt and trousers, his head at an awkward angle to his shoulders, almost as if avoiding recognition. One side of his face had healed so that it looked like the bark of the bloodwood marri. The lids of his left eye were coral pink and wept and drooped and often it felt as if that side of his face was still on fire. It was the memory of the spinifex and bluebush fire he and his father had been caught in while mustering out near Daybreak Springs. A brown Akubra hat on his head. He called to the blue dog. 'That'll do Jock, sit down there.'

Jock sat, mouth open and long pink tongue hanging out, closed his mouth and began to scratch at something behind his ear. Groaned as he scratched.

'Hello Painter Hayes. Had any rain?' John Drysdale held out his right hand.

'Boss,' Painter said. 'No rain.' He took John's hand and they shook hands.

'The bloke upstairs has been trying us,' John Drysdale did not smile.

'Keep calling him, boss,' Painter nodded. 'It'll come.'

'Better be, let's hope so.'

Painter turned his head, coughed and spoke as John looked to Lew.

'This is Lewis McCleod, Mr Drysdale. You may have known his father Mac?'

'Can't say I remember him. How are you Lewis?'

'Good good Mr Drysdale.' Lew said and held out his hand. They too shook hands.

The land was silent, the truck's motor ticking from the heat of the motor. A pair of crows called to each other and after a minute, the metal creaking sound of the Comet windmill began. They watched the D-pattern tail swing away from the wind coming out of the desert.

'His father shore here,' Painter said, 'in the late thirties once or twice I believe.'

'He did?' Drysdale looked closer at Lew.

'First I knew of it Mr Drysdale.'

The circle of blades whirred, moving in the air. The wind lifted and the flukes began turning faster, and the familiar sound of the air and moving metal of the windmill.

'Anyway good to see you both,' Drysdale said. 'Mustered yesterday. Shed and yards full. Just the hoggets. Tally I have is just under twelve hundred head. More or less.'

Lew and Painter both nodded. 'Good good.'

'Three days I would say. Four the outside. Perhaps a week or so if it rains.'

The sky was blue for as far as they could see. No clouds, not one, just the wind coming out of the eastern desert. The windmill's pump piston began moving up and down, dry-hissing in the sleeve of its cylinder. A small dust cloud swirled away behind the woolshed.

'That is a hopeful condition Mr Drysdale,' Painter said.

'Never know,' Drysdale replied. He turned, as they heard horses coming at a steady run.

Clara Ruth Drysdale rode towards them. Nineteen and sitting a white gelding as if she had grown out of it, holding a big-bellied grey mare on a long rope behind her. The horses slowed, baulked a little to the walk and stopped in front of the men as red dust caught up and blew around her and over them. A team of lean mustering dogs loping behind her. They circled Painter and Lew. The head dog lifted his leg against the wheel of the truck, squirted a line of urine and ran over to Jock to stand and bristle in defiance. Jock's top lip lifted and he began to open and close his mouth. The edges of his tongue curling as he too snarled. A low growl coming from his throat.

She had dark brown eyes, freckles and black hair cut unfashionably short. Cheeks flushed brown red with blood and sun. Her father's old, worn Akubra hat, hole in the peak. It had come off her head and hung down her back by a cord. Waved a hand in front of her face at the flies. Smiling yet as the gelding walked back three more steps and began turning away from them. Touched his nose onto the upper jaw of the mare on the lead. Nibbled at the halter brow strap.

'We just having a bit of a wongi,' her father said. 'Bit of a chat here with the boys.' He turned to the shearers. 'You remember my daughter Clara, Mr Hayes? The image of her mother.'

'I saw your truck coming Mr Hayes.' She was almost shouting in her easy breathlessness. 'Good to see you again.' Pulled the white horse's head to the off side as she spoke to him.

'Miss Drysdale,' Painter said and smiled up at her. 'My you have grown. Good to see you. What are the horses you have there?' He recalled her love of the animals.

Clara waved again at the flies in front of her face. Glanced at Lew once, twice. He could not take his eyes off her. Three times now she had looked at him.

She looked back and pointed to the pregnant mare on the lead rope. 'That is our shy Pearl, she is in foal, well you can tell that by her look, and this is Tom, her half-brother who we had to geld as a yearling. Uncontrollable otherwise.' She leaned forward in the saddle and patted Tom's dappled white neck. 'Remember that Dad?'

The men all smiled up at her like they had heard something they didn't need to and were silent.

Painter spoke to her and pointed to Lew with an open hand. 'Miss Drysdale this is Lewis McCleod.

'Miss Drysdale,' Lew said. 'How do you do?'

Her face lit and she blushed and looked to herself; at how her loose work shirt was hanging off her. The jodhpurs tight on her thighs and a hole in the knee. The bloody flies all over her. A million of them. 'Hello there,' she said with the sudden confidence of boarding school. 'Good thank you.' Tom once again moving beneath her. 'And yourself?'

'I am fine thank you,' Lew said.

Painter watched them.

Drysdale was leaning back. Raised a hand and spoke. 'Clara, I was about to tell them that we will be doing the roustabout and pressing work in the shed. There are no shed hands coming.'

She shook her head. 'As well as mustering and penning? It won't work Dad. You should have got a shed hand or two. Goodness sake.'

'We have been having troubles. But they are sent to try us are they not?'

Clara looked at him as if he was losing his mind. 'I would rather shed hands were sent to help than troubles to try us. Or what about those awful bank managers. What did you call them, Dad? The assassins of hope? Like a weather forecast, you said they were. And we need to carry more sheep, Dad; have you seen the price of wool? White gold.'

Drysdale gave an uncomfortable laugh. Shot a quick look towards the shearers. 'Well,' he said, 'I don't know about that, girl.'

Painter coughed. 'We better get settled in then Mr Drysdale,' he said. 'We'll get over to the quarters?'

Drysdale, nodding, was about to say something when Clara spoke up. 'There must be wild dogs, dingo about, I saw crows before, flying up and jumping like they do.'

'Dog crows?'

'Beyond the highway,' she said. 'Like they were following you almost.'

They looked to where she pointed. 'Gone now by the look.' Tom walking backwards beneath her.

The land fell away to the red mile track and fence line. The Comet windmill and water tanks. A flock of white cockatoos walking in a wide paddock behind the woolshed. The earth, yellow and red brown and in places shimmering white to clear. A line of trees marked the Great Eastern Highway about half a mile away. They watched as a large articulated truck and trailer appeared in the distance and the sound of a powerful American motor washed in to where they were and then it was past them and disappearing away to the east.

'Going to Kalgoorlie I expect,' Drysdale said. 'The gold mines there.'

After she had eaten, the dingo rested a short distance from the highway. She had followed the road until she found an overhanging rock outcrop fringed by wax bush, smoke bush and gimlet saplings. She was almost invisible.

Her belly made liquid digestive sounds and the two rows of her teats had begun to itch. Her eyes drooped and she put her chin on her paws and slept. Flies touched her nose and mouth. Once she snapped at them. Waited, made a small groaning noise and relaxed, lay on her side. Lifted one paw to rub it over an ear; allowed the paw to slip and rest at the end of her nose. Sand moving in front of her nostrils as her breathing deepened. A small pup-yip and she slept.

She opened her eyes when the ground began vibrating. Raised her head, ears turned to the sound. All other noise was sucked away as the approaching presence came through the red earth towards her. Terrified, she crouched, ears laid flat to flee, and as the sound roared by she snarled and flattened herself into the ground, tail between her legs. Roadside bushes swayed in the air wash of its approach and passing. The heavily laden truck and semitrailer roared past on the highway. She began to tremble and then made herself as invisible as possible in the earth and waited.

The noise faded away. She stood and came out of the hiding place. Sidled to a clearing and sat in the shade of a karrik bush. Crows were stalking about, as if following her. She ran at them growling and jumped up as they flew off to land a few feet away and caw and waahdong their displeasure. She raised her nose. Tested the air.

Clara was speaking to them. 'The windscreen on your truck is broken Mr Hayes.' She squinted to look more closely at their vehicle. 'And it is dented on the front mudguard. Headlight gone too?'

Lew raised his head. 'I almost forgot. We found a joey along the way. Would you like to have it Miss Drysdale?'

Painter was staring at him. 'Hold on now son.'

Lew turned and walked to the truck.

An explosion of dogs and dust. Jock and Clara's head mustering dog were whirling into a fight. Snarling and high-pitched yelping. The dogs were spinning in the dust. A great tumbling, shaking dogfight and some of the other mustering team ran in and savaged Jock as the yelping continued. One of them had him by the hind leg and was dragging the leg out. Another big dog was attacking his flank. Jock yelping and tumbling in fright.

Clara rode Tom into them, bent low down on the neck of the horse and yelling to the dogs, growling at some of them.

'Get out of it King you blasted nuisance. Meg. Fleet, get. Stop it Boofy you bloody pest.'

John Drysdale walked over to the fight and simply booted his blue dog out of it. Jock ran, bleeding, carrying a back leg and yelping in pain, ears back and tail between legs, to the shelter of the ground beneath the woolshed.

Her father was pointing at Clara's pack of circling, victorious dogs. 'Why girl do you carry so many dogs?' Raised his voice to her turned shoulder. 'We don't need all of them. Girl? Well we do not.'

She did not reply to her father.

Lew was holding the joey. It was still wrapped and roped in the grey woollen blanket. Clara looked back at him as he crossed to where she was restoring order among the pack. She had dismounted and let the reins trail. Lew watched as she pushed the riding crop into the jodhpurs above her backside. It rode up like a flag as she bent.

Clara took a thin chain from a saddlebag and ran the chain through their collars and clipped that back on itself through the woolshed yards. Speaking to each of the dogs as she did this. 'Sit down there King. Yes you the boss. That will do Sky. Good girl Meg. Sit down Fleet. Behave yourself just now Boofy, you bloody fool of a dog. Dee you darling.' Sometimes she just said their names. Jess and Bill. Swift and Don.

Each of the dogs showed their obedience to Clara as she chained them. The senior dogs glancing at her with soft eyes and placing dignified chins on paws. The younger dogs tending to abandon all restraint and, in a frenzy of subservience, roll on their backs and wag their tails, desperately trying to lick her hand. Bill, still young enough to roll over and demonstrate his adoration by pissing all over himself.

Clara turned from the dogs and smiled up at Lew. Stood. 'What?' She stepped forward and uncovered the head of the young kangaroo as you would uncover the head of a baby. Gave a chuckle of delight. 'What have you got here?'

Lew was holding the blanket-covered bundle. 'You will have to name it Miss Drysdale. Especially now it belongs to you.'

Behind her the dogs, which had all stood, noses lifted and quivering, began to boom and bark as the scent of the joey came over them. Clara turned her head. 'Quiet,' she growled. 'King. Stop it.'

The dogs quieted and settled, watching Clara's every move, her every gesture. Tom was walking back again, dragging the reins away from them. Pearl moving with him, also backing away. Clara beamed as she examined the delicate head and face bones of the terrified joey. 'What a darling you are,' she whispered. 'Sweetheart.' Two fingers exposed the nose. The baby kangaroo was struggling in the blanket. Lew, smiling too, reached to cover its eyes. 'What do you think?' he asked, handing the bundle to her. 'Would you like to keep him?'

She took the joey and glanced at him. Put her hand into the blanket and felt between its legs. 'It's a her.' Wiped her hand on the blanket, blinked. 'A girl. What happened? How did you get her?' She laughed.

'Last night,' Lew shrugged. 'This one's mother jumped in front of the truck. You see what she did to it.'

The men looked at the truck.

Clara frowned. 'No.' Stroked the baby kangaroo between

the eyes. 'I should call you Mercy. But I think Gwen is better. Gwennie it is.'

Painter and John Drysdale came over and looked at the bundle in her arms. She held it and showed it like her own child. 'Meet Gwen, Dad; Gwen meet Dad. Mr Hayes have you seen little Gwennie?'

'Have I ever,' he said. Lew shot him a hard look.

Drysdale grumbled and patted Painter on the back. Spoke to Clara. 'Better let the boys settle in to their quarters. I killed a sheep for them. It's hanging in the cool room.'

Painter was rolling a smoke. 'Good good but we're right for tonight's dinner. I'm making a soup,' he said and looked at Lew. 'Any spuds, boss?'

'There is a sack of potatoes. Some cabbage and onions,' he said. 'I'll get Jimmy to bring you some fresh bread. Fruit preserves. He has butter too, fresh made from that little Jersey house cow. Velvet he calls her.'

'Jimmy?' Painter asked. 'Who is Jimmy?'

'Jimmy Wong. He is old Chung's nephew, you remember Chung? Jimmy come down from Broome when his uncle went home. Bloody good cook and gardener. General hand about the place. Y'know.'

Painter nodded. 'I liked old Chung. Used to be a miner too didn't he?'

'He did. Found a small vein at Thompson's Find I believe, when it ran out he worked for the old man. Started as a laundry-man. Place ran a lot more head in those days and the old man reckoned the blacks were useless around the place.' He glanced at Clara. 'Do you think, Clara, you could give us a moment?'

Lew saw a shadow pass over her face. She stared at her father and waited a moment before she nodded. 'Yes, of course. I beg your pardon.' She walked across to Lew and held the bundle containing the baby kangaroo out to him. 'Here, hand this up to me would you please Mr McCleod? In a moment, once I'm up.' She retrieved Tom's reins, stepped into the stirrup and swung into the saddle. 'Righto.'

Lew passed the blanket carrying Gwen up to her. She nodded to him. Cradled the blanket. 'Pearl's lead Mr McCleod?'

She took the lead from him and sat for a moment, looking at each of the men.

'Excuse me Dad, Mr Hayes and Mr McCleod. I had better get back to the house. Thank you for little Gwen here Mr McCleod, that was so thoughtful of you. Dad, I'll see you at tea?' Kicked the gelding on. The left-behind dogs had stood and were watching her; some of them whined. Clara turned in the saddle and spoke to the dogs. 'That will do. Quiet now. I'll be back for you.'

'Hasn't really been herself since her mother,' Drysdale said. 'Her mother would have delighted for an armful of that joey you blokes brought here. They would have laughed over it together. What to feed her. What hat to wear.' He shook his head. 'I'll never get over it. She explains things to the bloody dogs. I'll be back. Lord, as if the dog knows. That will do?'

She had ridden away towards the homestead. The air was hot and bright. After a bit it was as if she was floating above the ground.

'A fine daughter Mr Drysdale.' Painter said. 'You must be very proud.'

'Capable,' Drysdale said, looked at Painter. 'Image of her mother. Same school y'know, those girls.'

Painter closed his eyes as Drysdale spoke again. 'But too many dogs. She keeps too many damn dogs.'

'You probably right boss. Too many dogs.'

The dingo bitch was standing beside the highway. Thin long white rectangles marked the centre of the road. She looked west where the men had come from and then east where they had gone.

Almost a photograph, a painting: a solitary dingo standing beside the metal road that stretched into the shimmering distance. Heat waves in both directions made the horizons indistinguishable. No clouds, the sky enclosing the land for as far as you could see. Enclosing her. The enormous sun, sister, was the fire and the light, impossible to look at. It would blind her, she knew.

She sniffed the road and placed a front paw on the hot metal stone. Raised it, took it back, and studied the other side. Whined then and retreated into the run-off hollow beside the road. She ignored the scattered detritus and crossed into the cover of karrik bush. Began to trot in the direction the men and nyarnyee had gone. East to moon rising, sun rising.

Fresh water springs along the way to the place her clan had

always gone to whelp. Old hunting lines in the river courses and rocks; layers of dry caves and shelter. A place to get water and meat and she would not have to cross the road. The demon crows followed her.

The shearers quarters, a pair of long corrugated-iron buildings joined by covered breezeways, facing north and with wide verandas. The ceilings were high and the rooftops had double hip gables with hinged skylights in every room to let the heat out, the light in. Cedar lilac trees along the west side ensured shade in the summer afternoons and later, when they shed their leaves, sun in winter.

Five dormitories ran off from the breezeways, each large enough to sleep eight. At one end of the quarters a cookhouse, and at the other an ablutions block with hand-operated Simac pumps, Baird showers, baths and washing tubs. Four galvanised and two wooden scrub boards hanging along a wall. Cracked yellow blocks of Sunlight soap and pale wooden duckboards.

Outside the washhouse, covered water tanks with galvanised pipes positioned from the gutter lines to the top of the tank to catch winter rainfall. Clothes lines, wire strung between poles, wooden pegs in a wire basket. About ten yards from the back door of the washhouse, three narrow outhouses, also made of corrugated iron, whitewashed doors propped open to air and to indicate they were unoccupied. Inside the long drops, a wooden seat with the pear-shaped hole cut into it. A spike to hold squares of newsprint on one wall and a bucket of quicklime with a ladle on the other. Graffiti on the walls written in pencil, blue and red raddle chalk sticks. Names and initials. Comic figures of genitalia; women's breasts; the results of the 1947 Melbourne Cup. Hiraji, Fresh Boy, Red Fury. And: Go you grey bastard you 12 to 1. £60 12 /- 6d. Somebody had written: I wish I was in Bendigo. Underneath: I wish I was in Lana Turner. A path along the front, edged with white rocks. A hand-painted sign: dunnys and an arrow.

They drove the truck up to the front of the quarters and got out. Painter walked up the steps onto the veranda carrying his swag over his shoulder, canvas carry bag in the other hand. Lew followed, also with his rolled swag on his shoulder. Both wearing hats pushed back and identical in walk, the cast of their bodies. Painter's leather-heeled boots on the boards. Lew, barefoot with bowyangs. Dust rising.

They found rooms opposite one other and unrolled the old kapok mattresses onto the wire and iron bed frames. Returned to the truck and carried in two boxes of supplies for the kitchen.

Painter had wrapped the kangaroo tail in a towel. He sniffed it and laid it across a large butchers block in the corner of the cookhouse. Nodded and took a Green River skinning knife from the box of supplies. Found a steel and began to sharpen the knife. 'Smells good this tail Lew,' he said. 'Better for a day. Sweeter the meat.'

He stopped sharpening the knife and cleaned the block

using white vinegar. Tested the knife with his thumb, laid the tail out across the block and drew the blade along the length of it. The skin lifted. Almost no fat, just dark red meat and white ridges of bone; some cartilage. He ran his thumb along the underside of the skin and peeled it back. Took a handful of the skin and pulled it from the tail meat. It came away with a dry, tearing sound.

'I need some flour and lard son. Salt and pepper.' He dropped the skin into a bucket next to the block, wiped the blade clean. Took a meat cleaver and chopped through the joint cartilage, separating the tail into eight pieces. 'Always spare the tip of a roo's tail for good luck.' Painter said. 'Like the parson's nose on a chook. Some call this the governor's cock.' Painter flashed him a smile, repeating what he said, almost in explanation. 'The governor's cock.' Wiped his hands. 'The old ticket of leave boys told me that story.'

'You told me that before,' Lew said.

'You want to get that underway?' Painter looked at a blue-green Metters Number One stove. Next to it a large wooden box filled with kindling and three small blocks of wood in a wall recess. 'Need to cut some more wood too by the look of it.'

Lew found some newspaper in a cardboard box, screwed three or four sheets into loose balls, fed them into the grate along with some kindling. Lit it and soon had the fire going. He placed his hand on the stovetop, waited and took it off. Smoke began seeping out of the chimney vent into the kitchen.

Painter was peeling onions. He looked at Lew with an expression asking what is it?

Lew checked the air-vent setting. Opened the stove's fire

door. Smoke billowed into the kitchen and he quickly closed it.

Painter coughed. Wiped his eyes.

Lew opened the windows, ran outside and stepped up on the bonnet of the truck. Hauled himself onto the corrugated-iron roof and disappeared.

When he got back to the kitchen, Painter had washed out the sink and filled it with water from the tank. He dropped the onions in the water. The smoke had cleared and the clean fire smell of the stove had begun to fill the room.

'Birds' nests in the flues.'

Painter nodded to him as he continued preparing the food. 'Bring in some more wood son. And make sure that Coolgardie safe is cleaned out and set up.' Indicated with his chin the square box with hessian sides on the bench near a window.

Lew picked up the safe and took it out onto the veranda. Gathered some water from the tank and poured it into the flat galvanised tray on top of the safe. He soaked strips of cotton and laid these down the sides over the hessian-covered wire mesh. Carried the Coolgardie safe to the shaded south corner of the veranda, and stood it where it would have best access to any breeze.

He found the woodpile and began to split the larger blocks. The steady rise and fall of the axe; the clean snap of the blade and the split. How, he often thought, he was the only one ever to have seen the pattern of the wood. The axe rose and fell, chips flew, and the smell of the dormant resin came up from the split eucalyptus. His shoulders worked and he felt the ache and pressure across his back from the spinal connective muscles. He had once spent eleven and six on a copy of *Gray's Anatomy* from a secondhand bookshop in Claremont. The fine line drawings fascinated but the names meant nothing. *Splenius capitas*; *lumbodorsal fascia*. Words that excluded, and he became content with you are just a shearer, you idiot, what do you expect? Keep going, Painter had laughed at him, saying don't worry mate, it'll be all right in the morning.

After about twenty minutes he stopped. Sweat was running freely and there was enough firewood for now. He gathered up an armful and carried it towards the cookhouse.

The smell of frying onions and meat as Lew came in. He took the wood to the stove, bent and stacked the split blocks neatly in the wall recess. Checked the stove, added another two lengths and closed the firebox.

Painter replaced the lid of the camp oven and lifted it to the top of the stove. 'That's just the go son, fry the tail meat and onions first. Bring it to the boil and about an hour, we'll be right. Don't forget plenty of salt.' He bent and checked the fire in the wood stove. 'Two hours better.' Crossed back to the water tank and filled a kettle, placed it next to the camp oven on the stovetop. Lew handed him a tin. Tea written on the side in paint.

Someone with an accent called out hey roo in there, a gentle knocking on the kitchen door as it swung open. A small man with baggy blue shorts, a white singlet, cropped black hair and a big smile stepped into the room. He was carrying a bloodstained flour sack, a wire basket of eggs and a cut-down wooden box containing loaves of bread and jars of peaches, red peeled plums in water. Light of the Age Water White American Kerosene stencilled in blue letters on the side of the box.

He started laughing. 'Gidday,' he said to Painter, 'mate.'

They both stared at him. After a minute, Painter nodded. 'You must be Jimmy.'

'Yeah mate. Jimmy Wong.' Laughed as if everything he heard was hilarious. 'I come from Malaya, Perak State. Jungle Jim, Ipoh, you know it? To Broome. Then Uncle Chung he goes home to family in Ipoh and I come here.'

They continued to look at him. Painter seemed to be frozen, his hands still.

'Mr John sent me over with this supplies.' He laughed yet again. 'You know Ipoh? Mining town. Tin. Big dredges.'

'Jesus,' Lew said, his hands in the flour sack. Brought out one hand full of kidneys, a lamb's liver in the other.

'You know Ipoh?' Jimmy repeated, stared at Painter, a smile frozen on his face.

'No. I don't know Ipoh,' Painter said. 'No.' He had not taken his eyes off Jimmy.

Jimmy laughed. 'Good good.'

'Go on keep laughing,' Painter said and pointed at him. 'Like you got no fuckin' brains. Ask me if I know Ipoh again, go on you chink cunt.'

'Hold on now mate,' Lew said and stepped forward. 'Cut it out.'

Jimmy stopped laughing, stared at the bread and box of fruit preserves for a few moments. His chin lifted. 'I won't ask again OK?'

Painter nodded. 'Good. Well we cleared that up then.' A smile lifted his top lip. He waited a moment, put his knuckles flat on the table and bowed his head. 'Here we all are then.

Never mind eh Jimmy? You can't help it.' He held his broken nose between his fingers and sniffed. Felt about between his eyes. Put a thumb against what was left of his left nostril and blew green snot out onto the floor.

'Sorry about that.'

Jimmy looked at the floor. His face contorted. Then he looked up at Lew and waved his hand in a farewell or denial gesture.

Painter was grim faced. He winked. 'I'm getting on a bit.'

'I go now. Dinner for Mr John, Miss Clara. See you.'

Lew raised a hand and stepped forward. 'Righto Jimmy,' he said. 'Thanks mate.' Look at me not at him. Pointed an index finger to the side of his head.

Jimmy turned away quickly. 'OK, OK. I bring you more tomorrow. Cook. Okey dokey.'

They were quiet as they heard his feet on the outside veranda and the rattle of a bicycle.

Lew stepped to the kitchen window and watched as Jimmy rode up the looping gravel track that led to the trees surrounding the homestead. He could see the terracotta tiles of the roof. Long trails of wisteria vines and two redbrick chimneys. Jimmy was standing up and leaning forward as he pedalled. His white singlet and baggy blue shorts, Bombay bloomers. Brown sandals on his feet.

'This bread is still warm,' Painter said. 'There's butter too.' He was standing with his back to Lew at the table, holding a loaf. 'Fresh-made butter this bloke.'

Lew turned from the window. 'How come you had a go at Jimmy there mate?'

Painter was spreading the butter on a slice with the same butchers knife he had cut the bread with. Concentrating on his task. Ate the buttered bread. 'Dunno.'

'Painter,' Lew said.

'He is a fuckin' Celestial son.'

'What do you mean?'

'Chinese.'

'Yeah?'

'That's enough,' Painter said. 'Laughs instead of saying what he thinks.'

'Jesus cut it out mate. That's not our go.'

Painter was quiet for a bit as he continued to eat the bread. Because he had no teeth, he had to tear the crusts off. 'When I was a kid, son.'

'What?'

'When I was a kid in North Perth, I did some runnin' for Baldy Reid, bread delivery bloke. He had the Loftus and Walcott streets run.'

Lew, staring at him.

Painter continued to speak. 'Horse and cart. Paddy was the name of the horse and old Baldy'd be talking to the housewives with his white shirtsleeves rolled up. It was morning missus hello good morning. There I was running about like a blue arse fly, dodging the number 38 tram coming down Loftus Street while he was talking to the wives with his folded arms, calling out orders to me from the side of he's mouth…one of white and half of brown and how's the baby Mrs Jones? Big smile he had. Not too many teeth.'

'Like you.'

Painter's laughter.

'I reckon Mr Reid was doin' a bit of boxing out the ring with some of those old girls too, no doubt about it. Used to touch his arm, some of 'em. Leave it on there for a bit, y'know, and they would laugh with their mouths open like they was getting something for nothing.'

Painter imitated the housewives' laugh. 'Oh, *ha ha ha* Mr Reid you such a funny man. *Haa haaa ha.* You make me laugh.' He bent and touched his hands on his knees. 'Some of them, they would do just that, bend over and put their hands on their knees as they laughed, just like they were bowing to him. Laughter is always the first betrayal. Y'know? Balance the books with their cunts, not the first.'

Lew was shaking his head at Painter. This old man's story.

'Yep,' Painter said. 'One of white and half of brown and how's the baby Mrs Jones, and no fuckin' worries Mr Reid. Good on him. They sweet for an afternoon with Baldy Reid, a cup of tea and a slice of butter cake. Settlin' the outstandings, if you know what I mean? Only fuckin' outstanding thing about him was in his pants. Do what you can eh?'

Lew nodded.

'Well. That's Jimmy there. Doing what he has to, to get by. Making bread, laughing his head off whenever he says hello. Or his mother got hit by a fuckin' tram. No difference. He laughs and hates like a snake who he laughs for.'

'Righto then.'

'Righto?'

'Don't go on about it. There's no changin' your mind.'

'Y'know, I sometimes wanted those women to just stop

laughing at old Baldy like he was some sort of a good bloke. He wasn't, I can tell you. Dear old Paddy, the horse right? That bastard Reid used to knock him about too.'

'That's got nothing to do with it,' Lew said. 'Treatin' Jimmy like that.'

'Everything to do with it son,' Painter said and stared at Lew. 'I didn't want to believe in Jesus for the same reason. End up in China, laughing your cunt out.'

'Get away now. That makes no sense at all.'

Half an hour later they gathered their shearing gear and walked down a side track towards the woolshed. They wanted to prepare their stands and sharpen their cutters for the start of the next day's work. Towels over their shoulders. They had left the tail soup cooking.

Cirrus in the western sky like a red thrown fleece, scattered clouds and blue sky rising beyond them.

'Footsteps to heaven,' Painter said. 'That sunset there. Fine tomorrow, you good for a start before light, mate. Four?'

Lew, walking beside him. A bandolier of combs over his shoulder and carrying a Gladstone bag that held crepe bandages, liniment and plasters. Spare wristbands, a bottle of aspirin, a box of matches and a tin of Dr Pat's tobacco. He didn't smoke but he always kept a spare tin in case Painter ran out and they couldn't buy any more for while. Told Painter he was a cranky old bastard without any smoke. There was also a tourniquet, a bottle of antiseptic and Condy's crystals. Eyewash and a pot of Vicks. Emu oil. Goanna oil, a sterilised needle and suture thread. An arm sling and a pair of scissors.

'I'm good for four.'

At the front of the shed three enormous white gums. Here before Captain Cook, Drysdale had told Painter. Bark was peeling off them in long, pale shreds and hanging down like scalded skin or a half-shorn fleece. If they could talk, Drysdale had once said to him. Painter had thought him a little touched to say that. If the fuckin' trees could talk.

The first thing that struck them as they entered the closed shearing shed was the smell, a heavy nitric smell of sheep wool and dung and urine. The startled clatter of feet as the penned sheep shied away from them.

'Leave the door open will you son?' Painter looked over a catching-pen door. 'Don't look too bad,' he said. 'Two-tooth wether and ewe hoggets.'

'Merino? Clean?'

'Merino cross. Pretty clean.'

Lew found the Villiers motor which powered the sharpening grinder. He checked the fuel level and primed the motor. Pulled the cord to start the engine. The metal discs onto which the emery paper was attached started spinning, slowly at first, then more and more quickly, settling into a steady hum. Painter stepped forward, said thank you.

Lew walked to the shearing board and looked down the empty length of it. Sat on an old wool classer's high chair with flat wooden arms on which to write. A pen groove and an ink well. Ink spatters from a thousand tally books. Fading light coming in from the windows. Long white spider webs in the overhead drive wheels and porthole doors closed. The stained board worn into smooth hollows from the passage of countless sheep and countless shearers. Something like a barefoot boy was running a clacking stick along a corrugated-iron shed. He had seen large teams of shearers and roustabouts posing for photographs outside a hundred woolsheds. He had sat among them. Soldiers and miners too.

Only their two catching pens had been filled. All along the rest of the shed, the immensity of an abandoned space; the other pens, other stands, empty now and for a long time.

Lew stood and looked at the board as imagined angels flew: like white cockatoos passing porthole windows and Your Cheatin' Heart playing on a radio. Heard the constant slap and bang of catching-pen doors being opened and closed. This work, bright and real, of noise and high metal on metal come to be surrounding the swaying lines of shearers in their vests, wet with sweat; long padded trousers held up with the wide leather belts that flared on the back as support. Bowyangs below their knees and moccasins made from leather or wool-bale sacking and brown bale twine on their turning feet. They were ever stepping and pivoting into their work with impossibly long arms, and backs that straighten to finish and rise to step forward again and again and again.

'Tween dog and wolf,' Painter, standing behind him. 'You been looking down there for a while now son.'

'I was thinking about the old gangs Painter. The ten-stand sheds. Those men. Twelve, sixteen stands.'

'Something to see when they going. Been in enough over the years. Errowanbang in New South Wales had forty stands. Near Orange.'

'Forty shearers?'

'So I was told. Blades but.'

'In the same shed, all those men shearing at the same time? Forty of them?'

'That's the story son.'

Seeking the cover of scrub land, fringes and hollows, she ran. Mouth wide open, tongue wet and balanced, her body adjusting to the earth as she passed through the country, she was what she had become, a pregnant dingo bitch running.

When she reached open land or a space of cleared unfamiliar ground she stopped at the fringe. Lay down and lifted her nose. Listened, waited. Listened again to the wind and any birds other than the crows. She detested them, the dog crows, their bold derision. They would scavenge her kills and yet perversely taunt. Once, she had caught an old one by a leg, too slow to lift off, and she had relished the slaughter. Ate its head off down to the breast, like a fox would. That was her disrespect.

If she became content the unfamiliar clearings held no danger or were unavoidable, she made her crossing quickly without breaking stride.

The sun was high overhead when she reached the rocks where there was a path to the water of the old mothers' springs. Paused at the break in the scrub where a two-wheel dirt track snaked towards the gates. Smelled horse dung; saw the droppings and the lifted dish shape of hoof marks in the gravel. A riffled line of domestic dog prints in the middle of the track where they had followed the horse. Their spoor markings of urine and sun-white faeces scattered along their line of travel.

She backed away, retreating further into the smoke bush. Panting from the journey. She lay under the low branches and brush, waited, her eyes closing. When she woke, she approached the track again, lifted her nose, smelled something rotting. She stayed in the cover of the scrub and trotted to the fence. Waited and turned to follow the fence line to where the emu gap should have been. Followed the sandy hollow alongside the fence while remaining on the hip of it and came across the decomposing carcass of a wombat. The foul smell above the exposed rotting body like a green mist, something to be avoided. The gap in the fence had been repaired with fence wire and mesh. She backed away, the deadly silence terrifying.

Her need for water was becoming desperate.

Lew made his way to the motor room and found the Bentall generator in the fading light. He primed it and inserted a crank handle into the motor. Rotated it slowly then rocked the handle.

Read: Timing at ten degrees of crankshaft rotation. Rubbed his eyes.

It was darkening in the motor room so he returned to where Painter was sharpening his cutters. A circle of red and orange sparks flew around the old man's hand. When he finished each cutter he threaded it onto its wire. It was becoming quite dark in the shed. He glanced at Lew. 'You right?'

Lew shook his head in the gloom. 'I want to start the generator. Make sure the lights and the machines are working.'

Painter shrugged. 'Good idea. You want the lamp?'

Lew reached out. 'I need to check the motor. Attach all the belts.'

Painter walked to his stand. The ringers crib. Traditionally, the first machine in the shed nearest the door and press, where the best shearer in the gang shore. A stand of pride and respect, hard won. Fought for with numbers shorn. He handed the lamp to Lew. 'There you are.' He began shaking a small oil can on the box shelf near the catching-pen door. Checking its level.

Lew returned to the motor room and stood the kerosene lamp on a table. Used a gauge to measure and tighten the timing belt, opened, closed and opened again the fuel lines. Primed the motor. Painter had followed him and stood at the door watching. The light of the lamp in the corrugated motor room; the solid Bentall engine as certain as tomorrow or the Bank of England. A wide drip tray beneath it. Wooden cross braces and a green forty-four-gallon drum of benzene. Sheffield spanners and a line of screwdrivers on a pegboard wall. Spare drive belts hanging from hooks. Chains, Birmingham made.

Lew found the crank handle, positioned it and took the weight of the drive shaft, rocking the handle back and forth. His arms were marked with sweat and his hair was wet, falling into his face. A streak of black oil on his shoulder. 'The bloody thing better start,' he said and rotated the crank handle with a whipping motion.

It caught, paused and hesitated. Hissed, almost at a stop. He straightened and lifted the rocker cover. Pushed his fingers into the top and side of the motor, found the SU, adjusted a grub screw and the engine caught again and began to run. He waited for a moment, his head turned to one side. Then he grabbed a spanner and used it to push a number of long and short belts completely onto their conveyors. The mechanical connections in the woolshed bumped and began to turn, squeal and then the whistling, sweet sound of the belts running through the rafters. The greased gears of the shearing shed. He walked along a line of overhead rollers holding an oilcan above his head. 'There they are now,' he said as he walked and squirted the oil can. 'Listen to that?'

'Young Mr McCleod.' Painter watched him. 'No doubt about you.'

The movement of air through the shed and once again the sheep in the pens stirred. Painter switched on a bank of lights and the shed began to glow orange, sparkling as if unsure, and as the generator pulsed the light changing and increasing to a steady yellow white.

'Good.'

They returned to the main part of the shed and it was Lew's turn to sharpen his cutters. The woolshed now bright and well lit. Painter walked to his stand and connected the handpiece to the down-rod. He drizzled oil over the comb and cutter, adjusted the tension and pulled the rope to engage the running gear. The handpiece buzzed and he studied it for a moment, pulled the rope again to disengage the running gear. Repeated the process with his spare handpiece. Filled the oil can and stepped to the catching-pen door, leaned on it and looked at the sheep in the pen. Lit a cigarette, waiting for Lew.

Lewis finished his sharpening, turned off the Villiers motor and walked to his stand. He also went through his preparations for the following day's work. Testing the gear, turning the hand-pieces on and off, tightening both of them to suit the pace of the generator. He placed the Gladstone bag below the wooden shelf on which the oil can, chalk raddle and tar pot and brush were kept.

They heard the sheep in the outside holding yards begin to make panicked sounds. Lew crossed to a window, looked out.

Two hundred yards away she lay in the coming dusk amid the gleam of insects and settling dust, waiting for her eyes to adjust to the night. She had not had water for two days.

She had been to Winjilla earlier and attempted to dig beneath the wire. Came across the traps, the stink of death and poison all over them. And now she waited. Put her chin on her paws. The itch and quickening of her teats and coming here to their water, the only water, compelling her to rise, low to the ground and to approach the yards where the men held the sheep.

The packed number of sheep was as nothing. It was the water in the trough that she could smell. Broke into a sliding trot, a white shadow in the dusk. A sharp angle against the light there. Craving, she moved along the set of yards, slipped sideways between wooden poles, through the sheep to their undeserved water and the mob went berserk, sprinting away from her as if she was already killing them, climbing on each other in their fear to get away from her.

She reached the water, lay down and watched, waited for just a moment. Then rose and began to lap at the stone trough. Her thirst had been eating her as she was now eating the water. Backbone showing, rising with each gulp, tail between her legs, hollow bellied but for her womb, gulping the liquid into her.

The lights in the woolshed came on and she heard one of the men open a window and look out.

She heard them speaking. The noises they made. The same, old man young man of the monstrous light. Clouds crossing the meeka. She knew their smell. When her gut was almost full, she stopped drinking and lay flat. Waited.

The men were becoming unsettled. As if they wanted to move. To begin to come closer. She darted glances to where she could flee. Ears flat, belly low in the stony rut near the drinking trough. Death surged into her blood, giving her strength, savagery, and detestation of these men who made noises only of indecision.

Lay still and listened to her own heart, its slow steady beat, her shallowest breathing. Nose taking in the scent of everything. Her being began now to quicken as she heard the shed door slide open. The young man walking down the wooden steps and across the ground. He was carrying a kerosene lantern and the light swung in flaring circles across the ground as he walked. His bare feet on the sandy gravel. The great wash of his stink coming towards the yards.

Her hind legs bunched, back feet seeking purchase in the ground, ears flattened and her top lip lifted in a soundless snarl. Her tongue flickered over her nose, licked at her silent snarling teeth and gums.

He leaned on the top rail a few feet from her. Held up the light and looked to where the panicked mob was still scrambling as to be as far away as possible from where he was. He leaned further over the rail, looked beneath it and along towards the drinking trough.

The dingo exploded into sight and sprinted away from him at a dog angle, racing into the mob of scattering sheep, disappeared among them for a moment and reappeared, leaping up and running over their backs like a working dog. She flew over the top rail and stretched out running, away into the night. Slowing for a moment to trot and look back at him. Turning east and becoming lost in the scrub and darkness.

Lew reared back as the dingo bitch burst across the yard. Before he could recover she was gone. He'd dropped the lamp and it was starting to catch fire in the dead grass from spilled kerosene. He picked up the lamp and quickly turned it off. Stamped on the burning ground with his callused feet.

Painter called out from the door of the shed. 'You right son?'

Lew pointed. 'A dingo. It took off.'

Painter walked to the yards, also looking out into the darkness.

They turned as they heard the noise of a Land Rover pulling up at the shed. The motor died and the hollow sound of the door opening and closing. John Drysdale got out and walked up the ramp. He hadn't seen them. Slid back the door and a great yellow square fell out across the ground. The blue heeler Jock running behind him.

'Boss,' Painter called to him.

They saw him pause and look towards them. Then, recognising Painter's voice. 'Hayes?'

'We are down at the yards. A dingo been here, in with the muster.'

The dog ran down to the yards and leapt over the rail. Lew watched him. The hair on Jock's scruff was standing and he was growling and running in circles, nose to the ground, seeking out traces of the intruder's scent.

Drysdale walked to the yards. 'Smith that old dingo shooter come down from Thompson's Find, far as I know, he laid poison baits and a trap or two at Daybreak Springs. Might have flushed a few out.'

Jock was growling and whining as he circled.

'Clara was right about those dog crows then. Can't have a dingo about. No. Get here to me Jock. That'll do you.'

Jock jumped back over the yard rail and sat at the man's feet. 'I heard Smith also cleaned up a big mob at Yate Valley station. I'll get him onto it in the morning.'

They all looked out into the darkness to where she had gone.

Drysdale nodded. 'Nothing we can do tonight. What time you getting a start in the morning boys? We got the pens filled. Should see you right for the first run.'

'About four we reckon,' Painter said.

'Good. Six for first smoko.'

He straightened and walked back towards the Land Rover. 'Night boys. Here to me Jock.' Jock ran to him and leapt onto the back tray of the Land Rover.

'Night boss.'

*

When they returned to the quarters, Painter served the kangaroo-tail soup which they ate in silence with thick slices of bread and butter. Once they finished, Lew heated water on the stove and shaved some soap into the sink to wash the dishes. 'What do you reckon about that wild dog?'

Painter shrugged. 'Old man Smith'll get rid of it.' He took a jar of preserved peaches and held them up. 'These look all right Lew. Be good with a bit of milk.' Nodded at the door.

Lew walked outside to the veranda and returned with the bottle of milk Jimmy had left in the Coolgardie safe. They sprinkled white sugar on the peaches, poured in the cream from the top of the milk and ate, sucking the sweet peach segments from their fingers.

'Sounds like he's been busy,' Lew said as he ate. 'Old Abraham Smith.'

Painter looked up at him. 'Oh yeah. You wanted to try that prospecting didn't you?'

Lew nodded. 'Yeah well I did. After we cut the shed out, what do you reckon? Head out to Thompson's Find.'

'See how we go son.'

Later that night they were still sitting in the kitchen drinking tea. Painter was rolling smokes for the following day and Lew was reading a 1952 *National Geographic* magazine by the light of a kerosene lamp. Looked over at Painter. 'There's an article in here about playing three thousand golf courses in fourteen lands. Good photos, look.' Showed the magazine.

Painter squinted. Nodded. 'I think I need glasses.'

Lew went back to reading. After a while he stopped reading and watched Painter. 'You ever play golf?'

'No.' Painter had about ten rolled cigarettes lined up in front of him. Tamped stray tobacco in at the ends of the cigarette he was holding with a Redhead match. Made a grumbling noise and started rolling the next cigarette.

Lew folded the magazine. Slapped his knee with it. 'Why did you used to drink like you did then? When you bad on it. Singin' out to who knows what. Fightin' all the time?'

Painter leaned forward, interlacing his fingers, and stared at Lew. He waited. 'I just liked it.'

'You did?'

'Yep.' He looked down and counted the cigarettes. Picked one up and put it in his mouth. 'Yeah I did. Loved it. Every fuckin' minute.'

'Cut it out Painter. There's got to be more to it than that?'

'No. No, there's not.'

Lew stared at him for a bit.

'Gettin' drunk? Goin' somewhere else.' Painter sighed. 'Like walkin' to China son and believin' in Jesus.' He lit the cigarette with a burning stick he had taken from the stove. 'Better than playin' fuckin' golf I would imagine.'

Lew was still holding the magazine. It was open now at the pages with photographs of perfect long green expanses. A man with a checked flat cap swinging a golf club above a white ocean cliff. Cocked hip, white leather glove on the left hand holding the club. Ventilation holes on the backs of the fingers. 'This bloke looks pretty pleased with himself. Bet he doesn't get pissed to bits,' Lew said. 'Calling out to Jesus and Mary and wanting to cut the world's throat. Who will wash my feet? You used to say that. Fighting everybody who even looked at you.'

Painter smoked, pointed at the magazine Lew was holding. 'No. He wouldn't, would he?'

Lew ignored him.

Painter stood, tossed the stick on the cement base of the stove and sat back down. Groaned. 'You know eh, my Mr Jesus never run away even when he could? Never did.'

'I know he never.'

'He was a tough bastard, Jesus was.'

'I know mate.'

'You reckon you know do you?'

'No. I don't know.'

'Those peaches were sweet weren't they? Jimmy give us the top milk too, good boy. Didn't scoop it off for the butter.'

In his dream he was approaching an old woolshed. There was banging and calls and yells coming from inside the shed as he walked up wooden steps towards the side entrance. He stood on the landing and slid open the heavy door. Stepped inside, and closed the door as someone was yelling: just in time for smoko mate. But it was he who was the yelling man. I am in time. One of the shearers had begun to hit a frantic, kicking sheep in the head with the side of a handpiece. Yelling at it, I will kill you. Stabbing it in the face. The wool classer looked at his watch as he came to the end of the board and rang a steel railway spike onto a suspended twenty-five-pounder brass shell case, called out: there are no blackfellas here; no they left of their own accord for the flour and the sugar and the tea. Dingo Smith persuaded them, oh yes he did. It was not theirs anyway was it? Just cause they danced here, doesn't make it theirs now does it? Now it's a safe place to swim. First run gone down boys…good work… Smoko time. Be careful now…mother's come home, ducks on the pond so watch your language.

The song on the radio loud in the shed. Your Cheatin' Heart. The shearers standing and leaning on the pen doors, wiping their faces with towels, hands on their hips and above their kidneys. Their heads began to nod; one turned to another and pretended to sing, using his empty hand to hold an imaginary microphone. Danced a small jig. The song and laughter lifted up in the shed. They walked tender easy, the shearers, wide shouldered, thin hipped and leaning back a little, rocking to the end of the shed. The song ended and a radio announcer began to speak about the weather and the possibility of rain in the wheatbelt around Koorda. A bushfire near the southwest town of Manjimup. Your Cheatin' Heart still yet playing on the radio. Hank Williams asleep in the back seat of a 1952 baby blue Cadillac. Good as gold mate.

He woke in the darkness of the shearers quarters. Looked around and saw nothing. Dream and memory merging.

Painter, in the opposite room, snoring. The building creaked in the wind.

His bladder was full and that was what mattered at the minute. He sat up in the bed, found a candle on the bedside and lit it. He made his way outside, carrying the candle with a hand cupped around the flame. When he opened the back door the wind caught the candle and blew it out.

Lew stood there and waited for his eyes to adjust to the darkness. It was a windswept night, desert clear and moon bright.

The wind making the immense throw of stars somehow colder and the third phase of the moon falling away to the west. He looked at his wristwatch, 2:15 a.m. He could see where he was now, the outline of the buildings, the truck and the sheep yards. The thrashing trees in the easterly wind. He walked around the side of the quarters to the trees and he urinated, ensuring his back was to the wind.

As he finished, he remembered the running dingo in the sheep yards. A shadow of long legs and open mouth, glancing back at him with indifferent, killer eyes. Her ears turned to him.

The wind chilled him and he returned to his room and got back into his swag on the kapok mattress. The warmth of that. Soon he fell asleep, dreamless yet somehow also aware that he was sleeping until the alarm clock woke him an hour later, 3:20 a.m. It was time to start breakfast.

Away from the water she had continued to run east. White under the waning moon, a crescent shade less than full as it was throwing light across the land, she ran until the moon was almost directly overhead; slowed and stopped, waited, listening to the night, smelling the wind, and began to circle back. It was the hunger. Cutting and recutting her tracks. Stopping often now and listening, her nose lifted. Coming around to the south, to be crosswind of anything that might be following. Waited and let the quivering knowledge of the night come into her. She began to hunt. Something stopped her; she stood still, lay down and waited.

Waited until she knew nothing. Now she could hunt again. She cut across her tracks, stopped and squatted to piss, ran on and stopped to defecate; scratched at the earth behind her. Circled and sniffed and again ran in a large backtracking circle to be upwind of where she had come from. Checked her leavings, others too. Rolled in them. The hunger hollowing her like the lack of water, she resisted the urge to howl, growling out instead her need, her whelps' unvoiced need, for hunting. Began once again to run. The calling in her blood. After a long time, she had returned to the homestead and shearing shed where she had been that night to water. The shed was in darkness but there was still a light burning in the big house.

She had travelled in a wide shape to be in the west of a holding paddock where a large mob of young hoggets had been mustered the previous day. The great bumbling stink of them came rolling to her. Their blind walking and touching comfort of each other's presence. The constant unthinking urination and shitting and lying down in stupidity on the bare stony ground. These creatures are what they are.

The bitch stood and slunk along the fence line. Waited and again slipped sideways through the rails. This time not to drink. This time to slaughter. She stopped. One foot raised. Her body focused, alone, absent from the pack run and kill. Took two tentative steps forward. Again raised a hunting foot, flattened her ears and head lowered below her shoulders.

A small ram hogget had strayed near enough to her to sense an unwelcome presence among them. He stamped a defiant front hoof and studied the darkness. A moment later, realising what was there, he let out a terrified moan and turned to escape.

The bitch was on the hogget in the time it took him to turn. Her teeth caught first along the eye socket and cheekbone. She readjusted in an instant and her mouth closed on his throat and she tore and bit down hard, strangling any noise, and they rolled over in the dust. She continued to bite down on his throat, shifting her body into the shape of her kill. Her back legs through and around his back legs. Without the pack, she had become the pack. Her patient eye lit in the shape of the moon watching. Deepened the grip of her mouth into the hogget's arched neck. She was waiting for the weakness. Waiting for the giving. Once it came she immediately ripped out his throat. Blood gushed over her face and she lapped at the torn hole. Paused, resting for a moment, blinked and relaxed. Panted, a bloody mouth and tongue. Waited, stopped panting and laid her chin on its ribs. The last of the hogget eased away and it became still. She crouched and bent her head between the back legs of the dead animal and began to rip and tear at its lower belly, exposing the intestines.

The pups in her belly squirmed. Aligned as they should be.

Lew rose, pulled on his trousers and shirt in the darkness. Remained barefoot, as always, his eyes becoming accustomed to the light. His feet silent as he crossed the veranda boards of the breezeway and opened the cookhouse door.

The kitchen was lit by three Coleman lamps and there was the faint smell of warm kerosene among the smells of cooking eggs, hot fat and roasting meat. Jimmy using a spatula to make small waves over the tops of the eggs. When the yolks were covered with an opaque film, he lifted the eggs from the pan and slid them onto slices of stale bread to drain. He would feed this bread to his beloved hens later.

Jimmy did not think in English. He thought in Malay. English was his third language. Penang Hokkien came after Malay. He bent to the stove and removed a tray of lamb chops and kidneys. The fat sizzled as he turned the cutlets and the rounds of kidney. He basted them with a spoon and slid the tray back into the oven. Almost done. Only take a minute. He laid thin slices of lambs fry and bacon in the iron pan in which he had cooked the eggs. Grunted to himself, bloody lambs fry; thinks he funny laughing at me.

He began to speak in Malay and after a while he crossed into Hokkien. A good language for cursing, the orifice of a pig sounding much better than in the English. Jimmy shook the pan and added another spoon of lard. Turned the frying bacon and liver.

'Jimmy,' Lew said, 'I just got up to light the stove. Thought I heard you in here.'

Jimmy turned to him and smiled. 'Mr Lew, I no see you there. Mr John tell me you start at four isn't it? I get you breakfast. First day. Big job. And you got no cookie. No good…You want a cup of tea?'

Lew nodded. 'Thank you.' He sat at the kitchen table. The lamp was hissing in the centre next to a pile of sliced bread and butter. An opened paper bag of white sugar. Glass jug filled with white milk. A bottle of Fountain tomato sauce. Lea and Perrins, the square bottle of HP.

'No newspapers sorry Mr Lew, you want I can bring you some from the house? Last week paper anyway.'

Lew waved a hand. 'No no,' he said. 'I never had a newspaper with my breakfast in my life.'

Jimmy laughed in bewilderment and looked at the table. Knives and forks had been set out. He placed a mug of tea next to Lew's elbow. 'Sugar *gula* on the table. *Susu*…milk too, fresh from cow. Sorry but don't put wet spoon in sugar OK?'

'All right Jimmy.'

'I mean it OK? No bloody wet spoon in sugar. It really piss

me off. Brown lumps pretty soon whole bowl had it, then, pretty soon, whole bag had it. *Semut*…ants coming anywhere then and no sugar for a month. No wet spoon in sugar OK?'

'Yeah, all right mate.'

The door opened and they both looked up as Painter came in and closed the door. He stood behind Lew and looked at them both, and around the kitchen. The smells and sounds of breakfast. The soft yellow lights and shadows of the lamps. Jimmy with a white apron and a white plate in his hand.

'Mr Painter.'

Painter looked at his wristwatch. 'It's three-thirty. Just after. Twenty to four.'

Jimmy indicated the chair opposite Lew. 'You sit. Cup of tea in a minute.' Began piling eggs and bacon, chops, kidney and lambs fry on a plate. He came to the table and placed the breakfast before Lew. 'There you are Mr Lew.' Slid the plate onto the table.

'Thank you Jimmy.' Lew took the bottle of Lea and Perrins and shook it over his eggs. Then the HP, poured a sauce line across the chops. Sprinkled salt and pepper and began to eat.

'Welcome.' He looked at Painter. 'Mr Painter. You want some *bleakfasts*?' Almost shouted the last word.

'Thanks mate.' Painter coughed and cleared his throat. 'Morning son.'

Lew paused from eating, took a sip of tea. Nodded to Painter. Reached out and took a slice of bread and began to butter it.

Jimmy placed the mug of tea in front of Painter. 'Sugar and milk there. No wet spoon in sugar please. I ask don't do it OK?'

'Righto mate.' Painter sniffed.

Lew paused from his eating and looked up as Jimmy turned back to the bench and spooned eggs and chops and bacon, kidneys, lambs fry onto a plate. Put it down in front of Painter. The plate bumped as Jimmy took his hand away.

'Thank you Jimmy.' Painter paused and, as was his habit, touched two fingers to his forehead, heart and each shoulder. Whispered a quick prayer of thanks. 'You and…by Your simple grace, amen.'

Jimmy was standing behind him, frowned, serving tongs still in his hands. 'Welcome Mr Painter.' Turned back to the sink and began to pour the excess lard from the pans into a large tin that had once contained apricots from Mildura. Began to wash the pots. Spoke in Malay and laughed in mock apology.

Painter picked up his knife and fork and began to eat. 'Done just right this *rams fly* Jimmy.'

Jimmy's shoulders tensed and he spun to face Painter, who was dipping a fold of bread into his egg yolk.

Lew was eating, not looking up as he forked the eggs, bacon and kidney into his mouth. Nodding. 'Good mate.'

Jimmy relaxed. 'Good,' he said. 'Okey dokey.' Laughed.

Painter and Lew continued to eat and Jimmy finished the washing-up.

'I have to go now. You get your own lunch. I make you mutton sandwiches for morning smoko. Mango chutney I put. Broome special recipe very beautiful. Ipoh spices.'

They both looked up from their plates and nodded. Lew said, 'Should be good then, the sandwiches. From Ipoh you say?'

'Yes Mr Lew.'

Raised their hands to Jimmy as he left. Forks still in their hands.

He poked his head back in the room. One hand on the door. 'They there.' Pointed at two brown paper bags on a side bench. 'There there. Morning smoko Mr Drysdale he bring more. See you. Thank you boys.'

They waited for a moment, listening to Jimmy's departure.

'You think you are a fuckin' comedian,' Painter said, 'don't you? Sandwiches from Ipoh.'

Lew was smiling as he ate his breakfast. 'What about you?'

'That was different.'

The dog crows squabbled over the remains of the bold two-tooth ram hogget but the dingo bitch had gone, carrying with her a back leg and some of the meat attached to the articulated spine and rib cage. Now she was resting in the lee of a small dry creek bed about a mile and a half from the woolshed. Flies covered the raw meat and she slept.

It was the smell of another dog that woke her. She didn't move, only her eyes opened and she watched him, then quietly opened and closed her mouth.

He was a deep red adolescent. A proud head, and now he crawled nose down with flat ears towards her. Downcast yellow eyes looking away. He adopted a subservient posture and stopped about five paces away. Began to inch forward, chin on the ground, his tail wagging stiffly.

She rose and the hackles on her neck rose with her. She recognised him: a strong youngster from a tough clan of kangaroo hunters. They had control of the land near the valley of the yate trees. A nearby wide flat valley with white quartz and clay banks. Screens of trees and winter water. The country was prized hunting land, sought out by mobs of heart animals and most lately the sheep and walking cattle. Everywhere they go, they are lost.

The yate valley clan was an impossible and dangerous confederation, hated to death by her and those of her remembered pack, two or three days away. The presence now of this young male was an aberration and something must have become very wrong in his world. She growled, showing her teeth, gnashed at him in a feint and her savage tongue flickered.

He licked at his lips, blinking and pushing his chin deeper into the earth. His tail stopped wagging. He lay on the ground and rolled over; his tail shot between his legs. Bent feet in the air, he swallowed and offered his throat. This was the complete surrender. A remarkable and entirely unusual display of desperation. Nothing like this had ever happened to her.

The bitch walked on stiff legs to where he had prostrated himself. Stood over him and ignored his pathetic throat but looked instead to where she thought he might have come from.

He had been wounded with a shot in the back leg on the point of the left buttock, blood streaked his fur down to the hock and inside pastern. His pads were torn and also bled. She looked away and back again. All the pads except the foot of the wounded leg.

She once again overlooked his wound and continued to study the ground he had crossed to her hiding place. Her nose raised above the stench of his terror. Ears pointed and straining for any hints of danger pursuing this idiotic pup beneath her. She knew he must have carried that leg, tearing as fast as he could away from whatever it was that had done this.

She bent her head and smelled at the blood welling up from the clean shot gash. Licked at it. Recognised it. The young dog flinched as she licked his wound, pulling his leg away. She raised her head and yet again looked towards the valley of the yate trees. The same thing had killed the black dog who had covered her. The sire of her whelp. The old man with a blue car and guns had shot him to pieces, dragged his body behind the car, gutted him. His open mouth and protruding tongue, pink intestines and flapping lungs becoming a smear of blood in the road. Wired his outstretched body to a boundary fence. She could smell him for days until the wind and sun dried him out.

After a few minutes the bitch bent her head, opened her mouth and took the young dog's offered throat in her mouth. He was passive, unresisting, a penitent and would never now be without her. He swallowed as his life was offered to her to take.

She let go of his throat, sniffed at him between his legs. Licked his penis and licked the wound in his back leg. Once again he flinched but as she kept her mouth there; he eased and allowed her to clean him as a mother would. She continued to patiently lap at the wound and the young dog lay, stretching his head out, and after a moment he blinked. Opened and closed his mouth. He was as pretty as a weaning pup. So far at least. If he could keep up; if he could run with her, then they would see. There would never be names.

They were on the second run of the first morning when John Drysdale came into the shed.

Chains of wet dust in the wrinkles of his neck. His Adam's apple moving up and down as he swallowed. The burnt side of his face had white zinc cream on it. Some dust had stuck to the cream. Lines the colour of bloodwood through the zinc. He stood at the end of the board holding a teatowel-covered basket in one hand and a black tea kettle in the other. 'I've brought the morning smoko boys,' he said.

Lew saw him first as he dragged a hogget out of the catching pen, called out above the noise of the shed. 'Painter.'

Painter, as usual, wearing his blue Jackie Howe and thick cotton trousers with protective padding sewn on the insides of his legs. Bowyangs below his knees and woolshed moccasins made from sacking on his feet. His broken face and muscular arms shining with sweat. Sheeps blood on his left, holding, forearm. Strong, ropy shoulders. The tattoos like a storybook you could look at but not read. He would say nothing or, at the most, I was drunk and I forget. His silence like a closed door. There was wool over the board and with no shed hands, the two shearers had been reduced to doing makeshift roustabout work.

Painter had his left fist pushed deep into the flank of the sheep as he made the last of the back-leg blows. Straight back, bald head shining. No place here for the weary. He looked up at Lew. 'What?'

Lew indicated with his head to where Drysdale was standing.

Painter finished the wether and pushed it out the porthole. Helped it on its way with a gentle backward kick. Turned off the shearing gear and slowly stood up. Wiped the sweat off his face and neck with a towel and looked at Drysdale with a smile and a look as if to say, please don't mention your fucking dead wife boss.

An almost silence descended on the shed. Still the clatter of sheep's feet in the catching pens; the lost blaring for each other, the calls and response of sheep in the tally-out pens. The Bentall generator humming in the engine room and the sweet running of the belts and air whistling through the rafters.

'I know Judith would normally bring it,' Drysdale said, speaking louder than usual. 'First smoko of the first morning. Bit of a tradition. Like Christmas. Or Easter.' He walked down the board. 'Things she would do now not done, see. Notice it more.' The sound of his boots heavy on the wooden floorboards and he continued to speak. 'I just wanted to say sorry how we haven't been ourselves lately. No pikelets. No Judith; no rain neither. Hah.' He tried to smile.

'It's fine boss.'

Drysdale nodded to Lew, who still gripped the hogget between his knees. Put his hands on hips and watched as he passed him and said, 'Thank you young man.'

This old bloke is not right in the head, Lew thought. Can't stop remembering. Repeating the need for rain like it's a prayer and apologising for her being dead. Bringing smoko on the first morning of shearing and saying sorry she died and could not help it. Jesus wept. Painter would hate this.

Painter waited and accompanied Drysdale until they reached the Ferrier press and placed the basket on a wool bale. The tea kettle on the floor.

Lew heard Drysdale say cups in the basket and saw Painter nod as the old man took off his hat and say something else while looking to his left to the open sliding door of the load landing. His hair was thinning and the top of his head a stark, shining white.

They walked outside onto the landing and Lew continued to watch as Painter took a smoke from the tin and he and the old man spoke to each other. Then another sound; it was high above them and they both looked up. A faraway drone and in the sky a plane. Small as a pen.

'Probably going to Sydney.' Drysdale's voice raised. 'Or Perth. You know Perth? She came from Perth. Went to that Claremont school there, Methodist Ladies. Like Clara.'

'Yeah boss I know Perth. Mostly East Perth, but. Never been to Claremont.' Painter put the cigarette in his mouth, cupped his hands around the match and lit the smoke. The tobacco tin still held between the knuckles of his fingers.

Lew pushed the unshorn hogget back in the catching pen

and wiped his face on a towel. He walked towards the wool press and the morning smoko basket.

Dogs were barking way out in a paddock and he saw Clara on horseback pass through a red screen of dust in the sheep yards. She was riding Tom and her team of dogs were working a large mob of sheep into the holding paddock. The sounds of her way-back and stop whistles. Fleet running so fast his back legs looked like they were going round behind his ears. Dee, sprinting to the head and turning them as sure and certain as she was. Good girl now. The surly hoggets veered back towards the shed. Clara dismounted and, holding the reins of her horse and the gate in one hand and a hat in the other, she ushered the mob into the outer yard. As they ran past her, some of the young sheep leapt into the air.

Lew heard her calling to the dogs: stop down there Fleet that will do. Stay Queen. Bring them on King. That will do Fleet. By God Dee good work girl. Down. Down. Beside me now. Speak up the Boof. And Boofy barking and running in circles to push up the lagging animals. Red dust rising around them all. She remounted once the gate was closed and pulled the head of the gelding around.

Drysdale put his hat on and turned his face away from them. 'Clara come here please, will you girl?'

Clara with a gloved hand held to her ear and head cocked to one side to hear what her father was saying. The dogs still working back and forth. Her lead dog King bounding over the backs of the mob to free a bottleneck at the inner yard gate, biting the reluctant faces of sheep, terrorising them.

She waved to indicate she understood and rode Tom to the

bottom of the landing and, again, dismounted. She was covered in dust, her face thick with it. Two clean lines of sweat ran from beneath her hat in front of her ears and across her jawline. Her father was speaking to her and she nodded.

'Dad. Yes Dad,' she said. Glancing at Lew, the dogs and ground; at her father's feet; Lew again. He counted. There were at least four times she looked at him and he at her.

Clara was shaking her head. 'I beg your pardon?' She put both hands on the pommel and, with a single swift motion, leapt up into the saddle; pulled the gelding's head up to walk back and come around to the off side. Whistled her dogs and did not look back as she rode towards the homestead.

'I'll take the Rover,' Drysdale said. 'Clara seems a little terse with me.' He spoke then to their silence. 'She is just a young girl Mr Hayes. Not getting any shed hands to help you blokes? Like the old days. Even the way I speak to her seems to annoy her. Hard without her mother.'

Painter shrugged. Smoke trickling out his nose.

He ignored Painter and looked at Lew. 'And by the way young fella, that dingo you saw last night came back. We found what she left of a ram hogget out in a southern holding paddock.'

'Bitch?'

'Yep, old Abraham tracked her. Reckons she is in pup too. Probably why she come so close.' He raised his hand, nodded and walked down the woolshed steps. 'He'll persuade her to move on, don't you worry about that. No more mutton for her.'

'Good good. Pups too.'

'For the best.' Drysdale said as he walked towards where he had parked the Land Rover.

After a few moments they heard the vehicle start and the whine of the differential as he backed out, changed gears and drove away.

Painter threw out the dregs of his tea.

'You press out a few bales mate, I'll sweep the board and start to sort this lot out.'

Lew was looking out the door towards the homestead. He turned away from the door and stepped up into the wool-filled shed.

Painter crossed to the sorting table and began throwing fleeces and skirting the wool. Testing the strength and colour and crimp. Working quickly to catch up. As he finished the skirt he rolled the fleece into a ball and carried it to the first of a line of bins along one wall of the shed. Returned to the table and threw the next fleece onto the table and began to skirt that. He moved along the edge of the fleece, removing the soiled wool and throwing it into the pieces bin. Ancient skills.

Lew took the fleeces from the bin Painter was filling and pushed these into the bale press. Filled one side, then the other. Climbed onto the press, jumped into the wool and stamped down the edges on both halves. He inserted three metal pins into one half to hold the wool in place and, using a pulley, raised that until it was upside down and swung it over onto the bottom half of the press. He took two metal bars with gear teeth along one side; eye bolts at one end and hooks at the other. Connected them to each side of the bale top and, using wire ropes, attached these to a ratchet with a long wooden handle. He began to tighten this, gradually pulling the heavy lid of the bale down to meet the bottom half.

'Pins,' Painter shouted from the sorting table. 'Don't press the bloody pins son.'

Lew stopped. 'Jesus.' He clicked the handle into safe and dipped his head to look. The fear of all wool pressers was to press the forgotten pins. But they came out easily enough, with only a slight bow in them. He had stopped pressing in time. 'Thanks mate.'

Painter raised one hand, said nothing and didn't look back. Kept working.

A flock of white cockatoos flew across the open loading door, between the shed and the track leading to the homestead. Lew could see where she had ridden to and he kept looking over in that direction.

It was around midday when Drysdale returned to the shed. He looked at the stacked fleeces in the bins and the two piles of belly wool and pieces in other bins. The already-pressed bales, piled high at one end of the shed. He nodded. 'You done well boys, thank you.'

'Would you like a cup of tea boss?' Painter said. 'There must be another cup somewhere.' He stood and looked towards the machine room.

'No no,' Drysdale said. He cleared his throat and scratched his shoulder. 'We have been a bit stretched.'

Painter nodded. 'Righto boss, we can wait for the cheque.'

'Cheque's good. It's not that.' Drysdale frowned and touched his burnt face, the tips of his fingers palping the remains of the white zinc ointment. He was staring at the floorboards and it seemed like a long time before he spoke. 'Y'know,' he said. 'If you lose a finger, with a saw or an axe, they reckon you can save it if you wrap it up in cobwebs and put it back on the stump.'

'What?' Lew glanced at Painter.

'I heard that too,' Painter said and nodded at Lew. 'The old spider webs got magic in them no worries.'

'The grass fires in the bush are tricky bloody things boys.' Drysdale's fingers exploring the edges of the scars. 'Don't ever underestimate them. No. Do you think it's true about the missing fingers?'

'Never know boss.'

Drysdale smiled, touching his burnt face. 'Could be, you think?'

'Could be.' Painter looked at the old man like he wished he would shut up.

Lew remembered his mother saying how she hoped her grief would cure her; it only made her helpless. His father asking what she wanted and she said you, and he said I can't promise you that. It makes you helpless, grief. 'It's all right boss,' he said. 'Don't worry.'

Painter opened his tobacco tin and took a cigarette he had rolled earlier. Put it in his mouth and lit it. 'You'll be right boss.' Painter looked at his wristwatch. 'We better get back to work but. Last run and bills to pay.'

Drysdale turned to go then stopped and raised a finger as if he had just remembered something else. 'I heard back from Abraham Smith. He's camped outside of Gungurra in that bashed-up blue Vauxhall of his. Said he would clean up that female dingo today.'

'Righto boss.'

'And I'll send Clara down tomorrow to help in the shed. She is a capable girl. Can throw a full wool fleece, she was shown how.'

Painter said nothing as he reached his stand and wiped his face with a towel. He stepped forward and opened the catching-pen door.

'Hello there my lovely,' he said to the sheep. 'I'm here to cut your stupid fucking head off.'

When she had cleaned his wound she stood and circled him, pissed and returned to the remains of her kill. He rose and touched his wounded leg to the ground, put weight on it and lifted it again. He hopped to where she had pissed and smelled the ground. Tried to urinate and almost fell over as he lifted his sound back leg. She paused from the chewing of ribs and watched him. This almost male almost fool of a young dog falling over himself attempting to piss where she had pissed.

She ignored him and went back to eating. He came to her and put his needy muzzle close to her mouth. She paused and watched him, her lips began to curl, she growled and the hair on her back rose.

His long pup tongue licked out towards her as he whimpered.

She waited and then she stopped growling. Something in her relaxed and after a while she stood up. He lay at her feet. Belly flat in the ground. Back leg extended, the shot leg. The only movement short, nervous wags of his tail.

She closed her mouth and moved a few feet away to place

her paw on the shank of the back leg of the mutton and begin to chew on the gristle. Looked at him to accept her invitation. The adolescent dingo rose and began to eat the ribs of the hogget she had left him. His sharp glances to check for her approval as he was stripping away shreds of dark red meat with his middle teeth. It was not so long since his milk teeth had fallen out. She did not care about that. Her approval came in the form of ignoring him. Allowing him to eat. Allowing him to remain.

It was later that afternoon when he came to where she was sleeping and woke her by making a whining noise and licking at her nose again. It was as he would have woken his mother.

She growled at him, showed her teeth. He backed away and after a moment his tail lifted, he pushed a front leg towards her. Another front leg and he turned his snout and made a feinting motion. Lifted his backside in the air, still favouring his wounded leg, but now he dipped his head, raised it, panting. Flirtatious. Made a playful advance, licked at her face with a long tongue. Retreated and gave a pup bark.

She raised her nose and ignored him, a mother's tolerance as he tumbled and fooled. He yelped, putting too much weight on his injured leg and her head turned quickly towards him. His attention changed then. He lay and began to slowly lick at the torn pads of his other feet.

It was not long after this they heard the sounds of a motor. The youngster's tail shot between his legs and he crawled to the shelter of a blue bush. The motor was revving and she heard the crack and graunch of a door opening.

The bitch looked up and the sky had already turned black. She had not heard the shot.

'Son.' Painter called out to Lew, who was filling the Ferrier press with rolled fleeces.

'Yeah?'

'Goin' back to the cookhouse to get our lunch. Be back soon, all right?'

Lew climbed into the press, began pushing wool into the corners with his feet. 'Painter?'

Painter paused. 'Yep?'

'You ever been in love mate?'

'What?'

'Been in love, y'know?' Lew kept pressing down on the wool, looking at his feet as he did this. 'Ever been in love?'

'You still thinking about that Maureen at the beach? The war widow?'

'No. Not really. I was thinking about how old man Drysdale doesn't know what's what with his wife dying. He must have loved her a lot. Y'know?'

Painter looked at him. 'I been in love,' he said.

'Any good?'

Painter wiped his mouth and face. Sniffed. His hands touching his pockets, searching for the tobacco tin. 'No.'

Lew stood still in the wool press and looked at Painter. 'No good?'

'No.'

'Sure?'

'Sure. We better eat.'

'Yep.' Lew stood in the press.

'You keep working. I'll be back soon.' Painter turned and walked out the shed.

When he returned he was carrying a large billycan in one hand and a teapot in the other. Two mugs hung from his fingers. Three enamel plates with high sides, spoons and a brown paper bag with slices of bread balanced on his forearms.

Lew was standing in the doorway, taking some fresh air. More wool bales, pressed, sewn and stencilled, stacked up against a wall. A curved bale hook protruded. 'What is it?' He nodded to the billy.

'The rest of the roo-tail soup.' Painter said. 'It's turned into more of a stew now, thickened up good. Jimmy made some dumplings to go with it.'

'Clara's pretty fond of that little joey I give her,' Lew said.

Painter looked at him. 'And we are eatin' Mum's tail. In here. What did she call it again?'

'Gwen.' Lew studied Painter for a moment. 'Would you eat Gwen?'

'Would I eat the nyarnyee Gwen?'

'Yeah.'

Painter laughed. 'For breakfast.' He was looking for somewhere to put the utensils he was holding. 'With eggs. You know I shore for a landowner once who used to give his kids a pet lamb to raise when they born. The children give them names like Snowy or Topsy, y'know? Round July August. Orphaned lambs y'know?'

Lew nodded.

'And the kids would raise up the lamb. Name them, feed 'em with a bottle.' Painter put the billy, plates and cups on a wool bale. 'You see how those lambs shake their tails when the kids feed 'em a bottle?'

Lew laughed. 'I have.'

'And then come Christmas time this boss would make sure the family, the kids eat the pet lamb for lunch.'

'The Christmas lunch? Turn it up Painter,' Lew said.

'Yep. The pet lamb with the darling name and the little waggling tail for lunch. Merry Christmas kids. We eatin' Snowy with the potatoes and mint sauce. Topsy's good with a bit of gravy.' Painter began to spoon the stew into the plates. Lumps of meat on the bone and potato, carrots. 'The boss said not to get attached to the meat on the table.' He sat on the bale, touched his forehead, closed his eyes and whispered grace, picked up a spoon and ate. Made a noise of appreciation. Took a slice of buttered bread. 'That Jimmy can make a decent loaf, I'll give him that; butter too.'

Lew was silent. He did not know what to say and his mouth felt as broken as the day Maureen O'Reilly had asked him his name and her mother called out to her, who is it?

Painter looked up at Lew and then indicated the plate on which he had piled the kangaroo-tail stew. 'It's good son. Eat.' He picked up a tail joint and sucked the meat from the bone.

Lew lifted his spoon and began to eat. Thought he'd be all right.

Painter nodded. 'That landowner had a terrible temper but.'

Lew poured them both a mug of tea. 'He did?'

'I saw him in the shed once with a dog that took a hen. It wasn't the first time this dog had chicken for Sunday dinner if you know what I mean.'

Lew nodded. 'They reckon once a dog gets a taste for chooks they can't stop.'

'Well this boss cocky, he dragged the dog in. Had him on a short chain and he took to hitting the dog on the head with the body of the dead chook, y'know? I'll stop you, he said to the poor bloody dog.'

Lew sipped his tea as Painter continued.

'He was holding the dead chook by the feet and he kept hitting the dog over the head with the body of the hen. Y'know?' Painter drank his tea and between waving his hand back and forth in imitation. 'Feathers started flying. He must have hit this poor dog two hundred times. And between each blow he would say, Don't. Eat. The fuckin'. Chooks.'

Lew was staring a few feet in front and nodding. He was smiling too because it seemed funny and he knew this was what Painter wanted from him. Him smiling at the story.

'He just kept hitting it. Blood and feathers, chook guts all over the dog's head. In the end all he was holding was two wrinkly little feet. You know the chook feet son? Got the claws on the end.'

'Yeah Painter, I know what chook feet look like.'

Painter drank his tea, laughed and made an affirming noise. Wiped his mouth and chin with a hand. 'Anyway, that's the same bloke who made his kids eat their pet lambs for Christmas dinner. Snowy and Topsy.'

'Same bloke?'

Painter nodded. 'Same bloke.'

'Who was it killed the lambs? Cut their throats?'

Painter looked up at him. 'Oh he did, cut them up too. Their mum put them in the oven. Roast pumpkin, potatoes. She made the mint sauce. '

'Jesus Painter.'

'I know son. You wouldn't wear this cunt as a brooch would you?'

'How did the kids turn out?'

Painter gathered the plates and spoons. Laid them on top of each other. Shrugged. 'Dunno. Who gives a fuck how they turned out? But that dog didn't take any more chooks, I heard that.'

Blood streaming down her face she ran. The shot had grazed her skull just in front of the ears and the young dog ran with her. He couldn't keep up but was doing his best on three legs. In his effort he was whining between every breath, every bounding leap to stay near her. Another shot; passing over them. It cut through the bush and, as it struck the wood, the dogs careered away at right angles. Yet another shot. This one landing about ten yards behind them. A fizzing smack as it hit the ground.

She did not know that when she was first hit she had simply sprinted at full speed for two hundred yards and dropped. Rolled over. Jumped and spun around as if bitten on the face by a snake. Threw herself over in a circle and then began to run again.

Old man Abraham Smith watched.

Children, he thought, sometimes children somersault when a heavy calibre takes them. They like scattering birds. He wiped his face with one hand. Seen a lubra do the same thing, shot through the head yet run like that bitch there, covered the hundred yards before she dropped, did a performance at the end.

The young dog heard him clearing his throat and remembered the terrifying sound and the sense of him. The hot smell of the shooting and the death of all his known family and he ran again for his life.

Abraham raised his chin to lift his white beard over his forearm and leaned across the roof of the blue car. Thumbed back the brim of his hat. His elbows braced. Aimed and squeezed off another shot. This shot passed over them. He opened and closed the bolt. He fired again, lowering his sights; the shot fell short and then they were gone. Again he opened the bolt of the Lee Enfield .303 to extract the spent shell casing. Removed the magazine and closed the bolt on an empty chamber. Put the magazine in his pocket.

Said nothing.

Jimmy Wong had been to the cookhouse. He had prepared an evening meal. A back leg of lamb was roasting in the oven and he had peeled a pot of potatoes and covered them in cold water. Another pot of cabbage and a bowl of skinned and segmented pumpkin. Gravy and mint sauce made.

They smelled the roast when they entered the quarters and Painter was standing in the doorway of the kitchen shaking his head when they heard the rattle of Jimmy's bicycle. Turned to see his wide smiling face.

'Mr Lew, Mr Painter.' He sat on his bike holding the veranda support post. His accent was still strong but they were getting used to how he spoke. 'Mr John asked me to do this.'

'Thanks Jimmy. Good on you.' Lew said.

Jimmy pushed himself off the veranda and turned the bike. Rode away calling out *hoo roo* and not looking back as he rode towards the homestead. *Cooooeee*, and his laughter.

Painter and Lew were covered in sweat and the greasy raw

lanolin of shorn wool. Sheep shit and blood. They entered the cookhouse, noted Jimmy's preparations. Painter took the pot of potatoes and put them on the stove to boil. He turned to Lew. 'You can wash up first mate, if you like.'

Lew nodded and walked to the washhouse. It smelled of artesian water and damp walls. He filled the Baird shower tub from the tank. Took off his clothes and stepped into the tub. Cranked the Simac pump and stood under the shower for a moment. When he was wet he used a block of soap to lather himself. Pumped on the wooden handle again and rinsed off. Twice more. He got out of the tub and began to dry his shoulders and face.

He was still naked when Painter came in and began getting undressed. Lew looked up and went back to drying himself as Painter filled another tub and threw his blue singlet, padded trousers and underwear in a pile.

Lew dressed in a pair of shorts and a cotton vest, an open shirt. He picked up his dirty work clothes and put them in the copper. 'You want me to wash your gear mate? I'm doin' mine.'

Painter was standing in the tub, wet from the first shower bucket. He was lathering himself with soap. Crossing his arms, knees lifted, eyes closed. 'Yeah mate, thanks for that. My turn tomorrow.'

'Righto.' Lew gathered up the pile of clothing and carried it to the copper. He poured in three buckets of water and lit a fire in the grate; used an old knife to peel thin flakes off a block of yellow soap and dropped them on top of the wool-greasy clothes.

Painter rinsed off and got out of the shower. Dried and changed into clean clothes. Rubbed antiseptic cream under his arms. Stained swabs of brown iodine on the cuts on his hands and arms. He too was wearing shorts. Then as usual he pulled on a clean Jackie Howe. Sandshoes, no laces, wet towel over his shoulder. 'I'll check dinner son. Put that pumpkin in.'

Lew raised his hand as Painter left and stirred the clothes with a wooden paddle for a while. As the water came to the boil, he took one or two steaming garments at a time and sloshed them into a bucket. Took them to the sink and scrubbed them on a wooden corrugated washboard. He rinsed them in a bucket of clean cold water and fed them through a hand mangle. Carried them outside to the clothes line and pegged out the damp clothes on the wire. He found the prop pole, and raised the line up in the middle. Secured the bottom of the pole. The wind took the clothing and he saw their trouser legs blowing out to the west. The easterlies coming in. They would be dry by morning.

The bitch ran, looked back and saw the young red dog running behind her. He was plainly exhausted and his face strained as he tried to keep up with her. She stopped and circled him. He came, slobbering over to her, licking at her face. She snapped at him to quiet. He lay down, panting on the ground. His whole body heaving with the exertion. The skin over his ribs, his frame lifting and falling. She too was gasping and her tongue was hanging, long, out the side of her mouth, she whined a yip yip with every breath and with the pain in her chest and for the danger to her whelp. His stupidity.

Then they heard the revving motor crashing and the car as it began to smash through the scrub towards them. The shooter banging on the outside of his door as he drove, trying to flush them into view.

The dingo bitch immediately sprinted away from the noise, yelping at the youngster to follow. Her sense of smell had been thrown out by the desperate flight; blood was streaming into her eyes. But she could still hear clearly and she ran from the terrible sound. Heard the yipping as the adolescent caught up and began running with her.

Tearing as fast as they could through the undergrowth, they came to a dry creek bed with banks about four feet high. She dashed into the creek, ran along the gravel bed for about ten feet and leapt up an embankment into the bushes on the other side. The young dog, following her, also tried to scramble up the bank but rolled back, his shot leg failing him. He tumbled as the car came crashing over the creek and bellied itself on the lip.

The shooter, howling now, was opening the door of his car. He began to point a rifle but he fell; the rifle fired and the shot went harmlessly into the air.

The bitch stood on the top of the embankment and yelped at the adolescent. He ran at the bank and threw himself up at it, his front legs clawing and his neck straining to get up. The one good back leg scratching frantically in the dirt. She reached down with her mouth and took him by the scruff, bit down hard and pulled him up. They fell together and rolled over in a tumble of legs. She was first to stand, waited for him to right himself and turned to look back the way they had come as they began to run through the brush.

Abraham Smith watched where they had run to. He sat in his car, rifle across both knees. Drivers door open and he had one foot on the ground.

It was getting dark and the shadow of the moon was rising in the east.

It was just after morning smoko the next day when Painter smiled and raised his hand as Clara came into the shed and walked to the board. He reconnected his handpiece to the down-rod. Drizzled oil on the comb and cutter.

'Miss Drysdale.'

'Mr Hayes.'

They both looked at Lew. He raised a hand and opened the catching-pen door. 'Miss Drysdale.'

'Mr McCleod.'

Lew caught hold of the nose of a wether hogget, twisted it down onto its backside, took both its front feet and dragged it out onto the board. He gripped it firmly between his knees, reached up and pulled the cord to connect the handpiece to the running motor, caught it up and began to shear. Took off the belly wool, tossed it into the board at her feet. Cleaned both legs and made three more short blows around the crutch along the back legs. Stepped forward and shore the throat, the head, the face and around the ears; across the poll and, turning the animal, began to sweep the handpiece up the flank and along its spine.

Painter watched him, took a few minutes, rolled a cigarette and said nothing.

Lew looked up from the long blow and said nothing.

Painter lit the smoke and then he too opened the catching-pen door.

Clara bent and scooped up the belly wool and threw it into the appropriate bale. She took a straw broom and began to clean away the offcuts coming from the sheep. Bent in attendance to the fleece as it came from the body of the hogget Lew was shearing. 'No second cuts Mr McCleod,' she whispered to him. 'Good work.'

He smelled white gardenias and he held his breath and looked at her mouth, which was smiling at him as she folded the fleece back and reached beneath the hogget's rump, freeing the bottom knot, to allow him access to the final blow. He nodded to her in thanks.

She walked the board between the men, retrieving belly wool, face wool, eye wigs. Sweeping dags and pizzle wool to one side. Bending to roll and gather up the wool. Sometimes she said, there you are, as the white fleece floated above and settled onto the classing table.

Lew was standing, paused with one hand on the catching-pen door. He was looking at her as he wiped sweat off his face with a towel.

'Mr McCleod?' She frowned.

'Yes?'

'Are you feeling well? You are staring.'

'My name is Lewis. Yes. You can…if you want to. Call me that.'

She looked at him. He was whip thin, strong and capable. He moved like a cat when he shore. Certain hands. Wet black hair and smiling mouth. She nodded, whispered, 'That's all right.'

He nodded. 'Thank you.'

'Not in front of Dad though,' she said. 'My name is Clara.'

'Clara.' Lew dipped his head in agreement. 'No. Of course not.'

They stared at each other.

Painter glanced over at them as he changed a cutter on his handpiece. He oiled the new cutter and stepped into the catching pen. Yelled to the sheep there: 'Hello.' Began dragging one of them out.

'Woolaway Miss Drysdale.'

'Oh.' She broke off from Lew and ran to pull the wool away from Painter's heels. 'Sorry Mr Hayes.'

The work went on. Dust rising up and blowing into the shed and the heat of the sun on the corrugated-iron roof come radiating inside. If you looked outside to the north the world was divided into two slabs of colour. Red and blue. The land and the sky. No clouds. No rain. Red land and blue sky.

Sweat arrived in veins, river-lines from the two shearers' ever-moving forearms and backs and shoulders. Strong necks and set jaws, blinking eyes and bodies never stopping. They were soaked with sweat, dripping.

Long white cobwebs blowing back and forth in the dark wooden rafters of the woolshed. You don't stop. No matter what, you don't stop working here.

Forever enclosed by tracks on the corrugated-iron walls, the black stencilled letters and names, spoor of other gangs, other pressers who had worked here. Their passing marks, like pissing on a tree. Station and farm names: Jindy Stn 1935 F/W 1200. R Horrocks Bellys & Pieces; I shore 250 Tobruk; 60 bales of

Glenburgh wool 1939; Jack Sorensen shore here. Wawoon and Gungurra. Carrington Homestead here. 79 H GRDC 2860. Spion Kop, JJS 300 strg wool lmb. Bimbjy Stn.

The dingo continued in a rough northeast pattern. The last shot had ricocheted away, smashing through the scrub. She still heard the old man cursing, heard the frustration and felt as if they would be safe from him. His howl of lament. His unhappiness meant safety. Almost victory.

The red dog was beginning to founder and she knew that she too was at the limit of her strength. They would have to stop soon to rest. They needed water. Blood, fat, meat. She slowed their escape to a steady trot but was determined to keep going for as long as they could.

They continued to travel, running on nothing but memories of themselves and themselves running until the young red dog simply stopped and staggered. He began to dry retch. His back arched, his body began heaving. Staggered again, this time backwards as if to sit, and fell over onto one side. Lay still and panted, legs straight out. One of his feet twitched. Drooling slime coming from his mouth. She returned to where he was lying and sniffed at him, licked his dry nose once. His eyes followed her, blinked and he then looked away to where they were running to. Away from her. She waited and then lay down near him. After a minute she lowered her chin onto her paws. Ears always cocked to the south. To where the shooter would come if he was going to.

It was quiet; the sounds of the still country began to return to her. The birds and nearby the noise of a lizard in the leaf litter and crunch of torn bark shredding from ancient gums. Wind come up out of the desert. Night coming also. Her head had stopped bleeding.

She looked over to the young dog and he had closed his eyes. His ribbed chest was moving in and out and she could see the sand grains and small sticks being disturbed in front of his nostrils. Quick breathing. His almost complete exhaustion was obvious. Death for him, close.

They finished shearing the next day just before lunch. Drysdale came and turned off the generator. It was late afternoon and the interior became empty and still. A long silence where there had been nothing but noise and movement. Lew noticed Painter speaking with the old man and them both looking at him and at Clara.

The swishing noise as Clara continued to sweep the board, ensuring everything was tidy and left as it should be.

John Drysdale stepped away from where he was speaking to Painter. 'You go back to the house please, girl,' he said and pointed at her. 'Good. Thank you.'

By the tone of his voice both Lew and Clara knew this matter was not to be questioned. Once again, she was being dismissed from their company.

'Go on now. Take your dogs.'

She shot a frowning look at her father, leaned the broom against the wall and left the shed.

The dingo stood and felt the giddiness, the ground whirling before her. She waited until it stopped. Took three steps, again waited. She needed to hunt and this need was as great as that to mate and to suckle; it was as if she breathed. Without glancing back at the young dog she put her nose to the ground and at first walked, then trotted into the long yellow grass. Soon she was invisible.

As her mother had taught her to hunt she now hunted. Mostly it was patience and listening. Stilling to become as the moving land, the earth, the smoke bush. Yate trees and gimlet, salmon gums, ghost and white gums wandoo. The hushing of her heart and quiet breathing and to wait and then to attack. Nothing else. It was nearly dark, but not to her.

She saw the bungurra as he saw her. The forked tongue flickered out at her and she leapt and bit down on its fat banded tail. Lifted it in the air and tossed it just as its sleek head came around to bite her. The sand goanna tried to flee into the darkening scrub but she sprang on it again and grabbed it behind its racehorse head. Her fangs crunched the vertebrae and the bungurra's head flashed open-mouthed, side to side. Its tail and body twisting in double-jointed reptilian fury. Twisting and hissing at her even as it died.

She drank its oily blood. Her whole body arching and absorbed with what she was doing. Tore the goanna's fat belly apart as it was dying. Swallowed the sweet stomach contents. The gorgeous yellow fat slid down her throat.

The body of the twitching bungurra goanna lay near her. Her belly began heaving from overeating and she retched but kept the food down. Her whelp roiled and she knew that they had been in hiding, tucked and still as she fled the killer. Now they were content.

Flies began. She took the lizard up into her mouth, its body hanging from her jaws, turned and began to trot back to where she had left the young dog.

It was dark, the night, when she reached him, he had curled closer into himself, changed his body shape. His nose to his tail. His breathing had slowed. This was a good sign. She dropped the half-eaten goanna near his nose. Walked backwards and lay down.

He woke and sniffed at the meat in the darkness.

She watched him as he began to lick at the hunt. Once she would have killed such an adolescent from another clan. Now he was taking the oil seeping from the fat of the bungurra. He rose on shaky legs and began to eat, gulping at the pale meat. He vomited. Paused and ate again, like a pup with undigested meat regurgitated for him. A mother's feed. She stretched and began to fall asleep. The first of the two moons rose.

Lew followed her out of the woolshed and stood on the landing.

She had reached the yards where Tom was haltered to a bottom rail next to a circular cement water trough. A saddle blanket and saddle on the top rail beside him. The bridle on a post.

'Clara,' he said.

She ignored him and took the blanket and put it across Tom's back. Turned to the saddle. One of the stirrup irons slipped and got caught as she lifted it. Lew was standing in his moccasins. Heavy cotton trousers, bowyangs. His upper arms, white in the sunlight as always, covered in cuts and scratches. He heard her curse as she dragged the stirrup iron out of the fence and turn to him. Her arms full with the heavy stock saddle.

'Lewis,' she said eventually, looking at him with a raised chin. Tears in her eyes.

Her team of dogs had aligned themselves along the yards, seeking out any scraps of shade. Lying down, heads up, panting and blinking, watching her every movement. Every gesture. All with open mouths, pink tongues dripping.

'I wanted to thank you,' he said, 'for all your help.'

She looked at him a moment longer, glanced at the dogs and stepped to put the saddle across Tom's back. Stood on tiptoes to free the iron from the seat and the twist. 'That's quite all right,' she said as she knelt under Tom's belly, her shoulder into his side, and retrieved the girth strap. Retreated again to her boarding-school voice. 'I enjoyed the change,' she said. 'And you are leaving soon aren't you?'

'I don't want to.'

'No?' Clara stood and lifted the side flap of the saddle, found the buckles, aligned and tightened the girth. Said stop it to Tom who had held his breath against the tightening, waited for him to breathe out and pulled the girth strap tighter. 'Unavoidable,' she said. 'Isn't it? Your leaving?'

'You are very beautiful, Clara, I have not ever seen,' Lew placed both hands on his head. 'And I keep looking at you and you do too. At me. I know you do. I just want to say this. Should I even say this?'

She shot him a hard look, turned away. Gave a tentative smile, her eyes becoming big as she lifted the bridle off the post and stood in front of Tom, said Tom and let the reins hang over her arm. Placed the headband across his forehead while bringing the bit up and into his mouth. Insisted to him to take it. She reached up to ease his ears and forelock through the headband and quickly buckled the chinstrap just as he champed at the metal bit in his mouth.

'I don't have to go,' he said.

She could not look at him. Her breathing had become shallow. Shook her head and after a moment of thinking, spoke. 'It's all right Lewis. It is. Thank you, that was a lovely thing to say.'

Lew looked over at her dogs. 'They can't take their eyes off you. Not for a second. They are all in love with you.'

She seemed to jerk, involuntarily. As if he had said something that shocked her, and she placed her hand over the eyes of her horse.

Tom began to swish his white tail at flies. Shook his head and blew air out through his nose. The rattle of the bridle and bit.

She retrieved the reins and put them over the gelding's head, held them in the stiff hair of his mane.

'Come over to the house stables later,' she said. 'I have a filly there I'm introducing to the lead. A yearling and she is just something. Black, but she will dapple to grey, same blood lines as Pearl and Tom.'

'Where?'

'At the dressage yards, near the house. I'll bring little Gwennie down for you to see. I have made a carry bag for her to ride in, wait till you see her.'

'Gwen?' Lew frowned, remembered. 'The joey?' This feeling of wanting to laugh with joy as he looked at her.

'Yes, Lewis, little Gwen. You did give her to me, remember?' She glanced at the woolshed door behind him. 'Don't tell Dad or Mr Hayes though, will you?'

He nodded. 'The stables? No, I won't.'

The team of dogs had stood as Clara moved. Their panting

and pausing as they watched her. How they loved her. Waited on her, tails wagging. Whining for her to notice them. Two or three of them sat, not taking their eyes off her for an instant. Not an instant.

'Down from the house. Try not to be seen.' She turned, held the pommel with both hands, leapt and swung herself up and into the saddle. Her feet searching out the stirrup irons. Tom lifted onto his back legs a few inches and she used the pressure of her thighs to turn him as she took the reins between the ring and middle fingers. Bent her chin forward to check the buttons of her shirt. Whispered darling to Tom. And: walk back; behave yourself now.

She was, all the time, in motion, turning away. The unchained dogs up on their feet. Standing proud and obedient for her. He heard her whistle; they barked, whined and trotted out behind her, arranging themselves into the pack order of dominance.

King in front on her near side. Fleet on the off, narrow eyed, glancing across at King to ensure he remained a little behind. A younger male ranged slightly ahead and Swift rounded on him and tore at his face in a short savage attack. The running order was restored and the dogs ran on, high wagging tails and open mouths behind their mistress. Sky looked neither left nor right. Her belly was full of pups again. Heads and tails, six maybe seven.

Clara raised a hand without looking back at him and kicked Tom into a slow canter. Her straight back and hips moving already within the rhythm of the horse's gait. Tom always ran more proudly when she was riding him. His white tail thrust out straight as a flag draped. Just fine and showing for all to see. I am alive and almost a stallion, a gelding cut-proud. Look at me, look at my tail. This is who I was.

Behind them shorn sheep blared in the tally-out pens. He did not know he heard them as he watched her. He could still see her arched back and the rolling movement of her backside controlling the sweet canter. He asked Painter's Mr Jesus, the Man on the hill, the moon, the entire universe and everything he ever believed in for her to look back at him. Even the hope of rain and her dead mother to return. Just at that moment.

Look back at me, Clara. I would die for you.

And she did, he saw her teeth, her lifted hand. Twisting in the saddle, she called something back at him. Her flat hand now on the rump of the running horse.

'I can, Lewis.'

He breathed out, wanted to kneel on the ground but instead smiled as big as he could and waved at her. 'Thank you,' he called. 'Thank you, I would like that. I would.'

He turned to the woolshed and saw that Painter and John Drysdale had come out to stand on the landing and were looking at him and then to where Clara was riding.

'You right son?' Painter called to him.

Drysdale stared at him and the damaged red eye seemed to be glowing in the white ointment of his face.

The bungurra had brought strength to her legs and heart and lungs.

After an hour of lying near the pup, the bitch stood and trotted back the way they had come. She was cautious, stopping every few hundred yards to listen. Cut back across their tracks to be upwind of any followers. The helpless and staggered spoor they had left was obvious; easy prey to any. She studied their tracks and sat. Waited and began to tremble. Stood as the shooter seemed to call out to her…No, just the wind. She turned suddenly to bite at something that wasn't there and began to settle into the running: alongside old bitch dingos coming to the hunt, gone in the teeth yet always obedient to the pack.

She was alone now.

Casting about for scent she became almost certain the shooter was not coming. It was too easy. Now using the old looping pattern of travel, she traced their tracks back almost to the dry creek bed where the old man had shot at them. Through the bushes she could see the car, still stranded on the lip of the creek. She raised her nose, there was no sense of the man, he had gone. Listened intently. The car seemed still and dust had settled on it. Oil and petrol fumes surrounding it. Something was pulling her to go to it and examine it more closely but she resisted this. The spirit of her mother seemed to whisper walk back. Come away child-pup from this thing. Leave it.

She walked backwards silently and turned. Began to trot to where she had come from. Night was falling and the western star come up. The moon's consort and suddenly a shower of falling stars. The great cloudless sky turning flare white for a moment and then back, almost black. Second moon rising.

She was running across the flat land in the moonlight. Her face, her open mouth was as she was, unthinking. Of remembered wild dogs running free nearby, in the shadows. The land moving beneath her. The ground came first. After that her feet and eyes and mouth.

When she reached him, she saw the young red pup had scratched a hollow for himself and lay, nose to tail. The bitch ran to him and sniffed. Circled and tested the perimeter of where they were sleeping that night. She pissed and defecated and returned to her markings to smell them as if to reassure herself of their presence and the boundary of their being there.

It was high moon dark as she came back to the sleeping body of the adolescent. She pawed the sand to create also a hollow. Again circled, sniffed and then lay down. Her back to his back. She felt his warmth and the movement of his lungs as he breathed. The sinewy strength of his dog youth came into her. The beating of his heart.

The black filly was light on her feet. Her coat shining and it was obvious she had the thoroughbred in her. Nervous and quick to move, eyes showing as big as you like, she looked at you beneath a black forelock, pricked ears and already long mane. Thick black tail held high and strong behind. One white foot.

Lew leaned on the wooden rail of the circular dressage yard and watched Clara as she gently laid the rope over the filly's back. All the time she cooed to her, hushed her and praised her. Sssh now the good baby girl, just a little bit yes you are, I am not here to hurt you. We are going to be good friends you and I oh yes we are ssssh now hush darling. I know I know, little bit. Come come to me to me. Look here to me. Steady darling now.

Allowed the filly her natural curiosity. Tentative at first and quick to start, she approached Clara, stretched out a long neck and smelled her. Began to trust. Clara watched as the filly gently touched her chest with her nose, stepped closer and became more curious with the unfamiliar smell and rub. Her ears moving back and forth, she began to nibble at the shirt pockets. Clara laughed and the filly quickly raised her head. The rope fell away into the dirt as she threw off to her near side and spun, turning her rump.

'Would you kick me darlin'?'

The filly laid her ears back and cocked her near hip as if to kick.

'Now now…Go on if you have to, just a little bit, go on.'

And she did, kicked out first with her near then off leg then hopped and kicked out with both back legs.

'Both barrels. A fighter,' Clara said. 'All the better for it. You a killer horse?' She whistled for a while and waited. Whistled again and watched as the young horse seemed to think about the whistle. Her ears moving back and forth. 'I don't think so.'

Clara turned away from the yards to allow the filly time to settle. To show her as a mother would that sometimes she should be ignored.

'She loves you,' Lew said and smiled. 'Just like your dogs, she cannot stop wondering about you now.'

'We will see,' Clara said.

The joey Gwen was in a sack around Pearl's neck. Holes had been cut to let her back legs stick out. A straw hat on her head with more holes cut in it to allow for her ears.

'She feeding?'

'I have an old long-neck beer bottle we use for the lambs. A rubber teat.' She frowned. 'She has the scours though. I don't think Velvet's milk agrees with her.'

'Some bread soaked in the milk, a little condensed milk?' Lew was breathless looking at her.

'My mother had a recipe for orphaned kangaroos. A level tablespoon of Sunshine milk powder; two teaspoons of cornflour, an egg yolk and a pinch of salt. Ten drops of Lane's emulsion and about a pint of hot water.'

He wanted to keep laughing in her presence. This joy was the strangest thing. 'Lane's emulsion?'

'Should work. Jimmy is so funny,' she said. 'He pretends to hate Gwen, saying we will eat you, hah haha, but then I caught him trying to feed her some butter on his fingers and cooing to her. We hang her up near the stove where it's warm. In the kitchen.'

'I like Jimmy,' Lew said and smiled. 'I do. Painter does not.'

'Jimmy's a darling. Such a tough old bloke in his own way.'

She remembered Jimmy, speaking Malay, patting and stroking little Gwen. *Pagi bayi yang baik*: good morning baby. Holding her ear. So funny your ears, *telinga*. This way and that. Miss Clara this one better not do a *kencing dan tahi* piss and shit on my floor.

She stopped and looked directly at Lew. 'It was Jimmy who found Mum. She had got herself into the water tank with handfuls of horseshoes.' She paused. 'He told me she was waiting for me in a better place. That it was a blessing. And such things are just the shadows of angels; that my freckles are the kisses of those same *malaikat* angels, he said that to me. I know they are lies, but it was comforting somehow.'

They looked at each other and he seemed helpless with such words. After a while, she came to his rescue. 'She was desperately ill and in the end it was a blessing. I think Jimmy may have even helped her. He was so very kind. Are you all right Lewis?'

'Yep. I'm good.' For some reason his eyes had filled with tears. He had not wept since he was a small boy and had witnessed his own mother's grief. 'What did you make the pouch out of?' he asked, again nodding at Gwen.

'You can use anything really,' she said. 'This is an old chaff sack.'

He was nodding, silent, as Clara continued speaking. 'She seems to love it. Must be like being in her mum I suppose, the feeling of running muscles. The warm body moving. The blood surrounding her. Safe as you can get.' Clara looked away towards the shearing shed. 'Today's Thursday. When do you leave?'

'Next Monday.'

They heard Jimmy calling from beyond the trees that screened the homestead. 'Miss Clara? You there Miss Clara? Dinner time. I fill your bath. Dinner Miss Clara.' He lengthened her name so that Clara became Claraaah. Bath too; it became baaaath.

'I better go,' she said.

Lew nodded. 'Me too. I told Painter I was going for a walk.'

'I'll see you later Lewis. Hold out your hand.' Stepped forward, gripped his hand and kissed his cheek.

He held his breath as she took Pearl and stepped onto the rail and then slid onto her back. 'Fat girl,' she whispered. 'And as for you,' she looked at the black filly in the yards. 'We'll have a wongi tomorrow sweetheart my little bit.' The filly had come to the rail to watch them. Her nose between the rails.

Clara pulled Pearl's head around. 'Got to go.' Gwen's straw hat nodded.

Lew watched her as she walked Pearl through the trees

surrounding the homestead. At the last moment she looked back and waved.

He began to walk towards the shearers quarters, where he knew Painter would be already in the shower. He did not feel his feet touching the ground.

The young dog woke her when the half moon was directly above them. The night was black and he had stood and walked out and returned to wake her.

He was correct, they needed to move away from where they were now, to begin to cross the country again.

She rose from the warmth of her hollow and stretched. Pushed her paws out and lowered her hips, lifted her chest and neck. Her spine came alive, hissed life into her as if a snake, as if bungurra. Shook her body and panted once then stopped as the night was cool. Licked at the young dog; if she was not in pup she would have mated with him the next time she came into heat. That time, it made her there for any dog. The strongest or quickest usually won. Her nose rose off the youngster, taking the smells of the night.

He ran a few feet away. Stopped and ran back to her, licked at her face. She was being entreated to follow. She waited; this was the country he had come out of and it was no longer his country. Her reluctance allowed him to lead and he ran ahead, knowing he was circling to a long, tree-fringed valley, his nose in the air, ears forward for any sound. Something must be terribly wrong there.

They ran through the remainder of the night, only stopping twice before the sun rose, and they lay on the lip of an enormous salt pan. On the other side was the beginning of the yate trees.

The red pup whined and licked at her face. Turned to run across the expanse of the salt.

Lew and Painter walked up a ridge behind the quarters until they came to a plateau. The immensity of land the downs covered stretched out below them. Clouds were building and dry lightning flickered through the darkness to the north. The distant clouds occasionally backlit by flashes, the reflected colours of sulphur and bright, white light through them; minutes later, far-off thunder.

Lew knelt and built a fire in the sandy red gravel from dried grass and dead twigs. He used Painter's matches to light it and once it was going he rose and circled where they were and came back with larger branches. Fed these onto the fire and sat down. Northeasterly winds blew the bright flames sideways away from the storm clouds. Sparks flying away in the wind.

They sat on large rocks and looked to the north. Lew held the quart bottle of Saint Agnes brandy Drysdale had given to them to celebrate the completion of the shearing. Painter was looking at it.

'You should not,' Lew said.

'I know that son.'

'You might end up in Kalgoorlie like the last time. Naked on Hay Street with that whore's underpants on your head. You were fightin' outside the lockup for fuck's sake. They were white and green. Shiny.'

'As her cunt and Ireland. She was Irish, I remember that.' Painter was silent.

'Ireland?'

Painter reached out his arm with the blue ship and the naked lady. 'Give me that bottle son.'

They sat and watched the cloud formations to the north. A slew of dark birds across their front.

'The drinking when it's heavy drives you mad,' Painter said. 'I broke both my hands once just cause some cunt asked me to fill out a form.'

A sudden wind took and lifted sand. 'Those forms they give you. Can you read and write? The cunts.'

'What forms?'

'I don't know. I smashed all my knuckles punching a cell door. Both hands, that's the drinking when it's heavy. Electric ants over my back. I would see cats and dogs. Not the real ones, just shapes like cats and dogs and they talkin' too. Once I thought I was the Man on the hill, come back. The second coming mate, the Mr Jesus himself.'

'What happened?'

'Someone asked me to do a miracle.'

'And?'

'I couldn't.'

Lew laughed.

'No fuckin' miracles,' Painter said and drank. Shuddered as he swallowed. 'Sometimes I would shit myself and in the end just blood. Wouldn't wash for a week. Sometimes two or three.'

'I remember,' Lew said.

Painter put the bottle between his feet and began to roll a cigarette. 'Almost out of tobacco son. I might go to town with old man Drysdale. You want anything?'

'No, it can wait.' Lew was shredding a piece of wood in his fingers. 'How much smoke you got left? I got the Dr Pat's in the Gladstone if you want.'

Painter didn't look up and waved a hand as to indicate it did not matter. He grimaced, put the cigarette in his mouth and cupped his hands against the wind as he lit it. The blue smoke came out his nose and he stifled a cough.

'The other day, son, you asked me about love, remember? If I ever been in love?'

He raised the bottle again and drank.

Lew stared at him. Thought of Clara's mouth and smile when she saw him.

'Yeah I did.'

'Is it young Clara Drysdale? You shook on her?'

'It is, mate; yeah, I am.'

Painter smoked. 'You cannot go there.'

Lew made a noise of disbelief and wanted for some strange reason to say you're all right but didn't and thought instead of Maureen O'Reilly at Cottesloe. How she, undressing, said Peter and you, who is not you. How wet she was with his fingers in her. His thumb on her navel and her neck tasting of salt. Then, her heels on his hips and her cunt like a clinging oyster. She was thirty-seven and smelled almost entirely of sea water. That 1941 Shell Oil wall calendar. A Wilson McCoy painting above the months and day numbers. Girl with Clown Doll.

He remembered thinking that isn't you either, Maureen O'Reilly.

'Well,' Painter said lifting the bottle. 'Happy days.'

Lew watched him drink. 'Who is Mary?' he said. 'On your arm. I have seen her name for ten years.'

'What?' Painter's eyes were glazed and he was staring at the ground about three feet in front of him. It was a long time since he had taken a drink. 'Mary?' Held the bottle towards Lew, who shook his head.

'Yeah. Mary.'

'My wife.'

'What?'

'She could play the piano like nobody's business.'

'What are you talking about mate?

'My wife.'

'Your wife?'

'Yeah.'

A dark curtain of rain swept towards the remaining distant light. It would not reach them for a while. Another flicker of dry lightning through the clouds.

Painter drank. Shook his head and drank again.

'But I could never trust her see. She was a woman and she laughed all the time. Like the housewives on Loftus Street. Full of fucking lust they are. Never trust a woman son they'll break your heart. Went back to some steady cunt and took my breath away. My heart in her black hand.'

Lew walked to the edge of the flat ground. Looked out at the darkening land.

'No, no.' He would not look back. 'Cut it out. It was our father who left us. Took off. My mother become mad as a cut snake after that. He belted her up a few times too. Knocked out her front teeth. Made her deaf in one ear.'

Painter hadn't heard him. He was drinking.

Lew turned around, he indicated the storm to the north. 'We should have gone to Broome or something. Drilling for oil. Crocodile hunting. Done something different.'

'Well we didn't. Did we?'

'No.'

'No.'

Another far-off lightning strike, a bright upside-down tree, white roots in paradise and branches coming into the earth.

'Come on, we better get back,' Lew said. He kicked sand and gravel over the fire and held his hand towards Painter, who was holding the bottle to his mouth. One hand back on the ground, bracing himself, gulping the last of the spirit.

Lew pulled him up and helped him to stand and when he let go he staggered and dropped the empty bottle, stepped back on it and almost fell. It didn't break. Lew heard the squealing sound of glass on sand.

'Don't leave the bottle,' Painter said.

'What?' Lew picked up the empty brandy bottle and followed Painter who was weaving ahead of him. Plaiting his legs as he walked. He began to sing I Am the Bread of Life. 'And I will raise you up this day.' His words had become so slurred that Lew could barely understand him.

'Jesus old man,' Lew said and put an arm around his shoulder to stop him from falling. 'What are you singing?'

'Don't say Jesus like that,' Painter slurred. He stumbled forward and raised his arms as he fell.

Clara rose naked from the bath and reached for a towel. She stood still and thought, I will not think of him. The steam rising as she dried herself. I will not. He has to go and I wish he would. I will be fine. I wish he would because that would solve everything really.

All sounds somehow louder in the white-tiled and still bathroom of the old homestead. The kerosene lamp burning on a mirror stand. Dark wood and brass latches. She could see the lamp and the reflection of the lamp and the circle of light on the wall of the bathroom.

Clara stepped out of the bath, wrapped a towel around her waist and walked into the adjoining bedroom. Wet footprints on the wooden floor. Immediately his bare feet and hands came back to her…I keep thinking about him, the smiling shearer… Lewis.

She began to dress. White underwear. And she sat on the bed to put white socks and tennis shoes on her feet. Pulling the laces tight. How would I know to kiss him anyway?

She pressed her mouth into the hollow of her elbow and tasted the bathwater. Skin and fine white hair under her tongue. To feel his mouth on my mouth, what is it to kiss like this? Shook her head. Finished lacing the tennis shoes. Feet on the floor with a bump.

Remembered the mare Pearl being covered. The power of that surrender. I will be someone else again after that. You are just a shearer on my land, I am better than you. That stallion Blue Boy mounting Pearl. His great mottled prick and his crazed desire. The violence of their need for each other. Pearl had been ready for two days, running with her tail high and flexing wet labia. They call it horsing, her father said. Pearl, the girl, is horsing, look at her winking at us. She is ready to be covered.

After a moment of them watching, he said excuse me I should not have said that. She had laughed at his eagerness to explain what they were seeing. Daddy was usually silent about such matters, leaving it to mother.

An arched clumsy thrusting of his great cock and her simultaneous need and hatred of him on her. Ears laid back and nostrils flaring as he bit hard, her neck, and rutted at her. She, for a moment, allowed this dominance and of her need of him inside her. For her too, it was pressing, to be like this.

I am not a horse.

The shape of her knuckles in the white cotton. I want to hear his thank you Clara. To place food before him and he nod, not looking at me. His mouth as he said beautiful. Such large fingers. Her eyes closed and she began to hear her father's gramophone. He would be drinking brandy again and soon fall asleep. The music would eventually stop. That scratching sound would go for a while until the winding mechanism ran down. Violetta in Verdi's heart. My mother believed these stories were real. She would ask my forgiveness for getting cancer and dying. Apologising for her death, my mother, saying sorry darling girl. I am.

Clara dressed, pulling on a white skirt and pale blouse. Sat on the bed, waited while her heart slowed and she could smell again the hot kerosene of the lamp. The smell also of her mother's perfume. White gardenias.

Crossed to the mirror and looked at her reflection for a while.

She stood and walked out of her room. Closed the door and tiptoed down the stairs and along the east passage. A light under the kitchen door and the sound of Jimmy still working, cleaning the kitchen. The smell of bread baking. Vinegar and sandstone soap on the floor. Jimmy, yelling in Chinese at an American jazz song coming from the wireless. Perhaps he was singing.

She closed the back door and felt the cool of the night around her, crossed her arms and walked, head lowered, towards the shearers quarters. Why am I doing this? I cannot not do this.

Clara passed the stables and heard the soft, breathing nicker of Pearl. Her lazy feet across the ground and she crossed to her. Tom was in the next yard and he too lifted his nose and smelled her. Pawed the ground and walked the rail, the clicking of his shoes in the stony gravel. She saw him in the light from the moon and it touched his back moving forever. Beloved horses. The dogs stirred and she heard the suppressed yowps of King and Sky; chains rattled. Whines and yips of anticipation. Imagined Dee's silence, her knowing eyes.

'Is that you Miss Clara?' Jimmy's faraway voice calling from the back veranda of the house. 'Down there?' Jimmy was outside, standing holding a hurricane lamp high.

'It's me Jimmy.' She called back to him. 'Just checking my little pregnant mare here. Been a dingo about.'

'The dogs,' Jimmy said. 'The dogs will tell us if that dingo comes too near the house isn't it?'

'Yes Jimmy.' She knew, he knew.

'All right then Miss Clara. You okey dokey?

'Yes thank you Jimmy.'

'Ah.'

She watched as he raised a hand. Turned, head down, and re-entered the house. Repeated himself. 'Ah.'

Wondered if Jimmy was waiting for her to return. Her father was sleeping but Jimmy missed nothing. She kissed Pearl and breathed her in. The wash of the horse in her nose. The soft muzzle, velvet top lip fluttering over her face. A sister's kiss and I have no sister.

Tom was still walking in the yard. White tail swaying.

The shearers quarters were about a quarter of a mile from the house. She would follow the line of old white gums so as not to be seen. Fence posts ran along behind the gums. Squat and as thick as a man's body, leaning left and right. Sagging and broken barbed wire around them.

The night was silent with a storm somewhere. Iron in it. The taste of blood the same, iron in it. If you have ever bitten your tongue or sucked a cut, it will rain, her grandmother said. It was the superstitious old north-country beliefs, these things which informed her. Like not cutting your hair or fingernails on a Sunday or Friday. A field of potatoes failed due to having it, the other, while bleeding. When you put your shirt or blouse on inside out it must stay that way for an hour at least. It must have wanted to be angry with you, that which you put on your own very self, who would think such a thing? Onions falling from a string, a stillborn child.

When she reached the signpost: Woolshed and Shearers Quarters, she turned to her right and followed the curving gravel track towards the long bulk of the shearing shed. The quarters were just on from that. Enormous ghost gums spread against the stars. Her eyes had almost become adjusted to the night.

The dingo came to the young dog sitting below the crest of the valley of his memory. He was sitting and trying to be who he had been, howling for the absence of his pack. His nose told him of their dead and rotting bodies. The clan, splayed and wired onto roadside fences. There was no mistake, the shooting. They had been gutted, their intestines spilled out in rotting heaps. Their bodies chained together and pulled behind the blue car. Laying a wide scent of destruction and havoc. The hunting clan of the valley wiped out. Soon even what remained of them would be gone. He lifted his face to the early morning sky and cough-howled. Sat as if thinking and then lay down. Put his front paws out and placed his chin on his paws.

She sat behind him and waited. When he had finished whining he came and lay next to her. Something of the pup had gone and he was a more serious dog.

She, without expression, stood and turned from him. Began to trot towards a dry creek to the north.

After a while he followed.

A young ewe in the rocks at the southern edge of the clan's old hunting grounds. She was having trouble giving birth and the front feet and face of the lamb were hanging from her fly-encrusted vulva. She had instinctively sought solitude to give birth in this late and difficult time and had left the rest of the flock in the main valley. The dingoes discovered her and immediately attacked.

The dingo bitch bit onto the face of the premature foetus and tore it from the young ewe. The young red dog had simply collided with the sheep and tumbled her onto her side. She was struggling to get up, legs in the air. The dingos circled and snarled as the blue-faced lamb lay in a slimy mess and they continued to squabble.

Crows had appeared and were already approaching the scattered kill.

Lew heard a light tapping on his window. He sat up and listened. Lit a bedside candle.

Painter was snoring loudly in the room across the breezeway. The tapping came again. It was the sound of a small stone being rapped against the windowpane in his room.

Clara was standing there, her hand at the glass. He pushed the curtain to one side and raised the window easily on its pulley. Stopped midway and he heard the gentle bump of the iron weights in the sash.

'Lewis,' she said and turned her head to one side to look through the half-opened window.

He lifted the double panes to their full height. A slight squealing noise and again, the low soft gong as weight and counterweight touched. The night wind blew in. It was cool and smelled of a storm. Still cloudless, the moon was waning towards the half. He could see her face, the shadows and short hair.

'Can I come in?'

She took his hand and he heard her place her foot against

the iron cladding of the building. Felt the strength of her arm as she lifted herself up on his outstretched hand. One foot over the edge of the sill and in a moment she was inside. She was wearing a pale skirt and it had ridden up as she climbed into the room. Just for a second, he saw the full lengths of her muscular horsewoman's legs, white underwear between. She stood, and jumped slightly as she pushed her skirt down. Standing there close together, they had again touched. 'Clara. What are you doing here?'

'Lewis, I…' She stopped. 'God, you have bad breath. Have you been drinking?'

His mouth was open and he stepped back. Closed his mouth. Laughed at her honesty.

'Oh. Sorry,' she said.

'No.' He shook his head. 'I'll go and rinse my mouth. Brush my teeth.' He had lowered his head so as to not speak directly at her.

She sat demurely on the bed, smoothing her skirt beneath her bottom.

Lew was searching through his canvas bag on the floor. Found his toothbrush and a tin of Alligator tooth powder. Painter was still snoring as he padded down the boards to the washhouse. He brushed his teeth and returned to the bedroom as quickly as he could.

Clara was sitting straight backed on his bed. 'Painter is very loud isn't he?'

He nodded. 'The grog. Been a while since he had a drink. Your dad gave us a bottle of brandy. Y'know, to celebrate the cut out.'

He lit another candle, took the light and placed it on the floor in front of her. Unrolled a kapok mattress and sat on the bed opposite. The flame between them moved as he moved. He bent forward and interlaced his fingers, cleared his throat.

Clara was looking at him in the candlelight. She squared her shoulders, hands held in her lap. For a moment, they didn't know what to say to each other.

'I came to ask you something,' she said.

Lew nodded.

'Today what you said.' She plucked at the cotton of her dress on her knees. Smiled, opened her mouth, looked at him. 'If you meant it and if you would stay on after the shearing. For the wheat?'

'Stay on for the wheat?'

'Yes, you said I was beautiful. And didn't know what to say after that. It was,' she frowned, searching for the right word, 'tender.' Yes. 'And how you felt, trusting even. It was brave.' She reached out and took his hand. Her hand holding his, this bold movement. 'Shearer's hands,' she said. Their fingers slid together, intermeshing. It seemed the most natural of things to do when holding hands.

'There is wool growing between my fingers,' he said. 'Like an animal.'

'Where?' She laughed and turned his hand over in hers and pulled the fingers apart. Peering at them. 'Where?'

'No,' he said, laughing. 'I am teasing you.'

She pushed his hand away. 'Stop it.'

'I will stay on for the wheat,' he said. 'And I meant what I said.'

'Good,' she said. 'I'm pleased. Thank you.' She frowned, still holding his hand, began to examine his palm, touching the callused dome at the base of each finger. Squeezed his fingers and shook her head at him. Her fingers closed around his middle finger. 'But first,' she said, 'you have to go and see Dad. Ask his permission to see me. Take me out.' Folded shut his hand.

'At the homestead?' Lew asked.

'Of course. It is the right thing to do. His blessing, Lewis. It's important. And I can take you to Daybreak Springs for a picnic and a swim. Dad will appreciate it I am sure.' She leaned across and kissed him on the mouth. Again her boldness. The dash of a good horsewoman. A good woman with dogs. That intuition that cannot be taught. And then she was rising up while still kissing him.

She broke off and stood. 'I promise. Now, I have to go.'

In a moment she had turned away from him, climbed out the window and disappeared.

The window was still open and he stepped forward to close it. Could not close it, and then he did.

Lew heard rain on the corrugated-iron roof. He looked to where Clara would have gone. Walked outside and stood in front of the quarters. The smell of a thunderstorm coming in from the night. Occasional wet drops began blowing in, spattering on the veranda boards and across his bare feet. The rain clouds lifting and rolling across the face of the moon. Slate to black, scudding clouds building upon themselves and the night down towards the ground in the rising wind. The first real rain came next. Fine and then thickening to something steady.

He walked out into the yard, his bare feet in the wet dust. Reached out and cupped his hand to allow the rain to fall into it. This is something, and he thought again of Maureen O'Reilly, how when he came inside her it was like a thousand wild birds flew out of his arsehole and she arched her back, said something he hadn't heard before. His semen on the black oil floor. Her hand cupped above her knee. Saying, young men have so much. It's all over me, in me.

Sudden lightning flashes and the smashing crack soon after. There was no time to count, he turned and hurried back towards the shelter of the quarters. The wind came in flurries and the rain became heavy as he made his way along the breezeway. Painter's door opened and Lew saw a lamp burning.

'Raining son? A storm coming.' Painter stood at the door.

'Yeah mate.'

'Did I hear voices before? Someone here?'

'No mate you dreaming,' Lew said.

'I could have sworn,' Painter looked towards the sound of the thunder. 'Must have been the bloody brandy. You smell that?'

The rain. Lew laughed. 'Smells good.'

'Good as gold son.'

'Night mate,' Lew said and stepped back to his room.

'Night.'

'Tomorrow's Sunday.'

'Day off. Sleep in,' Painter said from behind his closed door. 'My head feels like a football at the end of a grand final.'

Threads of the rainstorm hung in the air the next morning and a double rainbow formed to the west. The brilliant arcs began to widen and fade and after a few minutes both of them had gone.

Lew had risen early, showered and dressed. He watched the rainbows from the kitchen window and drank tea. Ate toast and Jimmy's cumquat jam for breakfast and looked at his watch three times before he left.

The old homestead was built of local honey-coloured stone and the hardwood timber jarra-djarraly. The stones had been taken from the Daybreak Springs formations. Lime masonry cement mixed in a dry creek bed near the house. The roof was of terracotta tiles, the old Cordoba thigh tiles carted up from Fremantle docks. Took two weeks. Bullock carts then, camels too sometimes in the summer, they said.

As he approached the house, he could see the wide, dark verandas with canvas deck chairs and old tables. Piles of books and the pages of abandoned newspapers lifting in the breeze. Iron filigree: circle and star, fleurs-de-lis; lathe-finished veranda posts and dressed lintels. Five palm trees in a row and green lawns.

Along the west wall, windows large and low enough for a man to step into and out of. Akubra hats, an oilskin Driza-bone coat and two coiled stockwhips hanging from hooks next to a door. There was a snaffle bridle and below that a stockhorse saddle. Four tennis racquets on another set of hooks against the ancient honey stones. Wisteria vines coming into full summer leaf and shivering, they had claimed a southern hip and an ancient jacaranda in the front yard, startling against the blue sky, the mauve November flowers. Some had fallen onto the red gravel driveway.

Jimmy was coming out of a side door holding a galvanised bucket in one hand and a stool in the other. He did not see Lew and disappeared around the side of the building. A rooster crowed somewhere beyond a line of lemon trees. Jimmy reappeared, leading the small Jersey cow, must be Velvet. He tied her to a fence and sat down on the stool near her back leg. He placed the bucket beneath her, leaned into her flank and, using both hands, began milking her. He turned his head, saw Lew as he approached the front of the house. Raised a hand. 'Mr Lew.' He called. '*Cooooeee.*' The cow too had turned her head to gaze at him. She slowly chewed her cud.

Lew paused at the bottom of the steps. Debated if he should say to Jimmy nobody used cooee like that anymore. Or that he was terrified coming here. Shook his head. Not within cooee. I am not within cooee of being good enough to walk up these steps. Thought of Clara and the candle on the floor between them. The canvas and rubber smell of tennis shoes and the length of her legs climbing into his window. The glimpse of white underwear between. He took a breath and quickly walked up the steps, crossed the veranda and knocked on the front door. There was no answer and he waited. He knocked again and after a few minutes John Drysdale came to the door.

'Lew?' He frowned and looked at him and past him as if looking for Painter.

'Mr Drysdale.'

'Lew, you here by yourself?'

'I am.'

'Well, what can I do for you young man?'

'I would like to stay on for the wheat harvest and to see your daughter, Mr Drysdale. Clara. With your permission.'

Drysdale reached into his pocket and took out a hand-kerchief, wiped his burnt eye. Looked at what he had wiped off. 'I beg your pardon?'

'I would like to see Clara.'

Drysdale shook his head. 'Well she is not here at the minute Lew. She...' He paused. 'You want to see her? Go out with her? To dances and the like? Socials and engagements? The Gungurra Show?'

'Yes Mr Drysdale.'

He almost laughed, then looked at Lew again. 'Are you serious boy? No. Don't be bloody silly, it's out of the question. Listen to yourself. You are a shearer. Clara is my daughter.'

Lew stood there, not knowing what to say.

'All right?' Drysdale stepped back into the doorway and began to close the door.

Lew realised he was nodding in agreement with Mr Drysdale. Heard himself even say yes all right then as he turned and reached the veranda balustrade at the top of the steps. His hand was shaking. He saw his leg go out to take the first step down and his knee too was trembling. Didn't remember reaching the bottom step but as he held the post he suddenly took a deep breath and spat.

'Righto, that's the story?' he said and felt a terrible burning in his belly; opened and closed his mouth. 'I am a shearer here.' A humming behind his eyes and he clenched and unclenched his hands. The biceps in his arms seemed more sensitive and he wanted to take off his shirt. She kissed me and asked me to ask, should I have told the old man? Knew it would have made no difference. I have become, he thought, a coward.

Lew was about to walk off when he heard the faint scrape of the front door being reopened. John Drysdale's voice.

'Young man.'

Lew turned.

Drysdale's eyes narrowed. He looked down at Lew from the top of the steps, studied him for a full ten seconds. 'I,' he said. 'I should not have been so short with you just then.'

'Mr Drysdale.' Lew looked up at him.

'You were good enough to come to my door, I will give you that. And I am the son of a Kalgoorlie gold miner. He was a man, he told me, equal to any other white man.'

Lew was looking at him and holding the rail.

'You better come through,' Drysdale said. 'I should like to show you something…I'm sorry about before.' He turned into the house and left the front door open, walked through a long hallway and opened a back door, also left that open, framing it in a rect-angle of light, stepped onto a wide back veranda and disappeared.

Lew followed him into the house. The hallway floor, a long narrow Persian carpet. Wide, dark floorboards. A table with a brass top and a dried flower arrangement in a vase. Yellow light from a side window edged in stained glass. Photographs of rams, horses and wedding groups. A bullock wagon piled high with wool bales. Dogs and Clara. Clara at the Royal Show on a grey horse, ribbons and medals around her neck and her smile. Fami-lies at a beach. A group of workers, posed in front of a mine-head poppet: Great Western Gold Mines. Two football teams and a cricket eleven. Into the light.

John Drysdale was staring at a small grave. A beautifully threaded marble headstone:

Poppy Elizabeth Drysdale
Born April 30 1902 Died Aug 21 1906
Aged four years and four months. Safe in the arms of Jesus.

A posy of rusting flowers fashioned out of sheet metal was resting against the base of the headstone. A plaster dove, sun pitted and ingrained with red dirt. An Agee jar with the dried stalks of dead wildflowers and a white line around the shoulder where the water level had been. Next to Poppy's grave another larger and more ornate memorial. Fewer words, more swag and scrolling.

William John Drysdale
Born 1858 Died 1921
At Rest Now.

John Drysdale glanced back at Lew and then continued to stare at the grave of his father. 'Sixty-three and still looking for gold,' he said. Nodded as if agreeing with his dead father. 'Yes, you were.' He knew the young shearer Lew was standing respectfully behind him, but he kept looking at the graves as he spoke. 'A bucket of rocks fell on his head. I found him at the bottom of the shaft. He had twenty-four thousand acres of sheep and wheat and he still wanted to find the gold. Twenty-four thousand acres, can you believe it?'

They were both silent.

'Y'know Lew, we never spoke much. My father and I.' John Drysdale cleared his throat, leaned back, looked up. 'That rain storm last night was promising,' he said. 'We might be right now.'

'It was, Mr Drysdale,' Lew said. He had approached the fence and was standing alongside the old man.

'After Poppy died, I asked him why our God would take her like He did.'

Lew was silent, nodding, not knowing what to say.

'My dad, y'know, he didn't say anything for a long time when I asked that. That bloody impossible question. Seemed like years but it was probably only about five minutes or so.'

Drysdale paused and his head sank below his shoulders as he laughed. 'And then he said, did you hear Poseidon won the Melbourne Cup son?'

Lew nodded.

'Won the bloody Caulfield as well, the old man said, and the St Ledger. Bloody good horse. Still entire. Tommy Clayton the hoop. A great Melbourne Cup it was.'

Lew cleared his throat. He didn't know what to say.

'It was 1906. Tommy died from injuries he took from a fall three years later, 1909. Horse called All Blue fell on him, would you believe it? Took him four days to die.'

'Four days?'

Drysdale nodded. 'Anyway, after my father was killed, Mother went to her people in Adelaide. She put me in a Perth boarding school and a manager on the place until I was old enough to take over. Never was right after Poppy, never was. It was the end of her here.' Drysdale waved at the flies landing on his face. 'Tommy Clayton. Yep, the old boy said he was a top jockey until that horse fell on him. You know what entire means?'

'No Mr Drysdale,' Lew said. 'I don't.'

'It means they hadn't cut his balls off.'

Lew looked at the headstones. 'Like a wether? Or a barrow?'

'That's right,' John replied. He nodded to Poppy's grave.

'My little sister. I remember when she died. Snakebite. Big brown, must have been five foot. Over near the chook run. I was eleven.' He straightened and squeezed the top rail of the fence in his hands. 'Little Poppy. Still see her sometimes. Bugger it.'

'A brown snake, Mr Drysdale? The gwarder?'

'Yep,' he slapped his hat and hand against his leg, 'gwarder kill a horse. They can.' He cleared his throat, waited and continued speaking. 'I wanted to name Clara after her. Call her Poppy. But Judith found it too morbid. You have to let go of the past, she said. Judith was my wife. The cancer. Did you know?'

Lew looked at the sky. Cumulus cloud moving against the blue. 'Yes sir,' he said.

'That's her over there,' Drysdale indicated with his chin a small black marble headstone off to one side of the family plot. White writing. A mound of red soil. The rain from the previous night had gouged tiny run-offs. Dead flowers flattened. Exposed white stones.

'I see her,' Lew said.

Drysdale did not indicate he had heard him. 'How can you do that? Let go of the past. That's just nonsense. How can it not be what it was, and what it is?' He continued to speak, appeared unable to stop now. 'I will be buried here next to her. Clara will take over the place. My mother is buried in Adelaide. At the West Terrace cemetery there. She didn't want to be here.'

They were both silent for a long time.

'You can't go out with Clara, Lew. See her.'

Lew frowned and slowly shook his head in bewilderment. 'What? I'm sorry Mr Drysdale,' he said.

'Do you not understand?'

'No sir.'

'This?'

'The graves of your family, Mr Drysdale.'

'There's a gate around the side of the house.' He gestured to the right as he continued looking at the gravestones and markers, kept speaking, ignoring Lew.

'I want to stay here for a bit longer. This is where I'll end up. Go on now and have a think about it. You worked hard boy, I'll give you that, shore fine and clean. I'd have you back.'

Lew stepped away from the railing.

'But it's completely out of the question boy. You are who you are and there is no changing that.'

Lew did not notice Jimmy standing with two buckets, watching him as he let himself out through the side gate and walked back towards the shearers quarters.

Again, he tasted the bitterness of his stomach. His heart beating in his temple and at the end of his fingers. He had never felt like this since the day he had watched his mother weeping and holding the pillow over her face so he wouldn't see the bruises and missing teeth.

It was coming into night when they stopped. She turned to the north and lifted her nose into the wind. The fur across her back ruffled and she saw the black storm clouds coming. She felt the thunder beneath her feet before she heard it. Began frantically to dig. The young dog had stopped next to her and watched. She was using both her front feet and digging as fast as she could.

He began to imitate her. It was as if she was trying to uncover a rabbit burrow with young to feast on. She had made a hollow deep enough for her and he was almost there. She started pawing at the earth where he was, helping him. The black clouds began to squeeze together above them. Rain drops hitting the hot ground. Flurries of water in the wind.

They dug faster and both lay in their hollows, noses to tails as the clouds opened above them and it rained. The sky became a storm and seemed to be running from something as she ran from the old man in the blue car. This is her licking the young dog. Him licking her. She shook herself yet again as the downpour continued. The hollows they had dug to hide in began filling with water. The rain in heavy sheets.

They stood and waited.

Every now and again the dogs opened and closed their mouths and simply endured. There was nothing else to do but this. He would glance at her but she would ignore him.

When the storm had ended and the rain stopped falling they sniffed each other in reassurance. He, at a loss, looked to her to make a choice. She raised her nose and sniffed the air and saw the night beginning to close. They stretched, front feet out and backsides in the air. Wide jaws and then lifting their chests and flattening their back legs. Stood up and shook themselves.

Clara came for him the next morning. Monday morning.

Drysdale had taken Painter into Gungurra to arrange for payment for the shearing. They were going to a branch of the Bank of New South Wales. Painter had repeated that he needed more tobacco.

She parked the Land Rover outside the shearers quarters, walked to the door, knocked, called his name and returned to sit behind the wheel.

Lew stood on the veranda, pulling on a shirt. She told him where they were going. Jimmy had helped her make up a picnic.

'Your father told me I could not see you Clara,' he said. 'I asked him if I could and he said no, it was out of the question.'

'What?'

'Did he tell you why? Say anything?'

'Nothing really. He left this morning. Took the town car. Said he'll see me when he gets back.'

'What shall we do?'

Clara stared at him and laughed. 'Come on, I promised you a swim.'

'I can't...I never learned to swim.'

'I'll teach you then. A swim and a picnic at Daybreak. No one will know. Only Jimmy and he's a love.'

They drove across the dirt roads for almost an hour. She would glance over at him from time to time and smile but it was difficult to speak because of the noise. It was just the two of them and they had to shout to be heard. The rain had washed the land and it seemed brighter than before. Sparkling. The air clean and sharp. Even the birds seemed to fly faster and twist as if in celebration. Lew had the almost constant sensation of wanting to laugh as they drove. To sing, and he never sang.

She yelled that it, the world, describing with her hand an all-encompassing circle, was this. Our land and we are the only young people in the world. That he too was with her and the laughter was infectious and with the noise of the vehicle and the crashing through it, unable to be heard, anything and everything seemed easier to say.

In just over an hour they arrived at Daybreak Springs. They left the Land Rover at the gate. There was a curving path between the rocks and trees and she held his hand until they reached the banks of a freshwater pool. It was edged with large rocks, kangaroo grass and paperbark melaleucas. Clara unpacked the straw bags. The towels and a bottle of homemade ginger beer. Sandwiches in brown paper made with cold corned beef, pink with a fringe of white fat. Piccalilli relish, pickled cucumber and onions, tomatoes and a square of butter. She tied string around the bottle's neck and lowered it into the cold water.

'We used to come here when I was a little girl,' she said. 'It was known as Winjilla Springs in the old days, grandfather told me, but he renamed it Daybreak. Told Dad it was in the first light of morning when they found it. And now it's a safe place to swim.'

She bent down, took off her boots, overbalancing slightly as she did so. Dropped her hat on the boots. Stepped forward then onto a tongue of flat striated red stone which led to the water's edge. Squatted to study the surface riffle and reflections of the sky. Turned back to him, looking over a raised shoulder. 'Come on.'

Above the pool were great slabs of grey and stippled red boulders. A small waterfall ran between fissured dolerite rocks and fell into the pool. The sound of water falling into water. A quandong bush clung among the rocks.

She reached out and trailed her fingers through the water, stood up and walked forward into the pool up to her waist. The blue work shirt floated and she caught her breath. Gasped. Arms lifted and she laughed. Held her breath, closed her eyes and dived forward. Disappeared beneath the surface. After a moment she reappeared and opened her eyes, wiped the water from her face and looked at him. Lay back and floated, arching her neck, staring at the sky. Opened her legs and kicked out, swam out into deeper water. She lay floating, drifting. Her hands beneath her back moving and she lifted her hips up, legs rising.

'If you fill your lungs with air,' she said, 'they become a natural float and you will never sink. If you are ever in doubt, just hold your breath.'

'Hold my breath?' Repeated as a question. Smiling away like a fool and shaking his head.

'The trouble is when you have to breathe,' she dipped below the water, resurfaced. 'You sink.' Laughed as if this was the most hilarious of things. They both knew it was simply the joy of them being here.

Lew sat on the flat stone next to her hat and boots. The straw bag and picnic food she had covered with towels. He raised his hand and nodded. Clara swivelled in the water and swam, breaststroking out into the middle. Stopped, again floated on her back, raised her hand and waved at him. She began to tread water; pulled down and kicked off her jodhpurs; unbuttoned her blue shirt.

'If you come out to me, I will show you how to kiss underwater so no one will see us. You can close your eyes if you want Lewis. But not when you jump. Keep your eyes open as you jump, it's more fun to see yourself falling through the air.'

Easterly winds coming over the top of them from out of the desert country.

He looked up and saw the rocks surrounding the pool. The rocks are as ancient as stars and Clara is swimming through the impermanence of water. He frowned at the strangeness of such thoughts, heard a faint humming and looked up. High in an old paperbark, he saw a sugarbag beehive hanging from a hollow branch.

Suddenly knew there would never be another horse without Clara, or another dog without her. Another held breath or held hand, without her. And she waited now, for him in the water.

She reached down and removed her underpants. Kicking

her legs as she did so. Turned and swam out to the middle. The roundness of her white backside bobbing. Opened her legs and her hips as she swam, fine and light and perfect; naked she was. 'No one will see us Lew.'

He shook his head as he rose and began to unbutton his shirt. Took it off and lay it on the ground. Big, capable hands. He unbuttoned his trousers. Dropped them at his feet and stepped out of them. His body was ivory white. A barely visible patch of chest hair spread above his sternum and across his chest like the shape of a flying bird. He stood slightly hipshot for a moment. Lean and strong arms akimbo, wide shoulders and thin hips, iliac crests prominent. His penis growing to erection.

Clara nodding, he could see her wide eyes, white teeth, and she began swimming towards him. 'Come on Lewis,' she called. 'Just jump.' Her laughter of approval.

He ran and jumped. Suspended for a moment in the air. The naked man, arms and legs running, falling. Building wings on the way down, becoming almost weightless.

He plunged through the surface of the water and twisted, instinctively looked up. His arms suspended among a thousand bubbles and rifts. It was cold and free. Underwater. He opened his eyes and could see Clara's body, her long legs kicking and the dark triangle between them. She, diving under now, was looking for him. He felt her slippery arms searching, her hands sliding around him. Blowing underwater bubbles from her mouth as she reached for him and their legs and bodies came together. Clara was holding him and kicking so they rose to the surface and as they broke through into the fresh air, he would always believe the rocks began singing and trees nodded approval. But of course it was the wind you fool. And the sugarbag bees. They were drawing great breaths into their lungs and laughing at the same time. He was trying to remind her, saying I can't swim Clara. Shaking his head and laughing at her. Don't let go. She, recovering first, leaned forward and kissed him. Her mouth on his and as this happened he leaned back and they dipped just below the surface. He felt her soft lips and her tongue in his mouth and he did not care as they continued to slowly sink. Their feet touching the clean sandy bottom and knees bent they both pushed off from the bottom and rose, again to the surface. Their mouths still locked together, arms around each other. His leg came up between her legs. The heel of one of her feet high on the back of his thighs.

Breaking the surface, again for air; the sun on their faces. Her arms around his shoulders and he held her around the waist as her legs came around him. It was as if she was saving both their lives. They were at the edge of the pool, her shoulders against jagged dark rocks. Keeping him afloat. She groaned and let go of him, waited, studying his face. Pushed him away. Turned, found the edge and pulled herself out of the water. Lew watched her and the sun coming over the turning and bending figure of her, straightening and moving and looking down at him. Her hand held out to him.

He would always remember her like this, the hollow at her throat and her beautiful breasts swaying down to him. Two small skin rolls in her belly, hip and thigh muscles tightening; her wet black pubic hair shining in the sun. How pale her skin and her feet so flat on the rocks. Her gentle voice. 'Lewis come on.' Biting her bottom lip and glancing away, just for a second, to her left.

They made their way, naked, through the rocks towards the cave.

He looked up to the formations surrounding the spring and the bor trees with the long white spotted stamens called mirlen, and saw from the corner of his eye other lean men who were not there. Bearded men imagined, watching them while standing, resting on one leg holding thin spears as balance and then looking towards the shining plains for meat. Pointing and taking the colours from the air around them to the bokadje line: the horizon. These old persuaded men speaking among themselves of all men and women. And how our overwhelming desire for each other was the desire to be alive.

She was kneeling and lighting a candle that had been left in the entrance. Turned to him and gestured with an extended hand towards the paintings above them. There were small stones that had been used to grind ochre. The remains of other ancient fires, charcoal. Animal bones. She whispered, look. And he smelled her as she raised her arm to point. The painted figures made him hold his breath.

He kissed her moving jaw. Her finger touched the Southern Cross and Western Star. The candlelight guttered and went out. He felt her turning to him and her arms around him. The paintings watching them in the dark. 'I dreamed of you,' Clara said. 'All my life.'

This intensity of longing for each other. There was nothing else.

The dingoes rested from the remains of the storm and the night running and woke in a grey light. Storm clouds to the west and yet an occasional flicker of lightning as the front moved towards the coastal land.

She walked out to some rising ground above a flowing creek. Stood at the highest point and watched the country from which they had come. After a while the adolescent joined her and they waited. The bitch shook herself again as the last of the black clouds rolled away.

They continued east, always east until they reached a ridge above a long fence. A long wire barrier the white men patrolled and constantly repaired.

They settled, bellies into the sand, and lay side by side and watched as a line of weitj came hurtling at the wire, running in that way they have, great shaggy coats of feathers moving side to side and their big dangerous legs whirling, crossing the ground in a seemingly effortless roll. The tiny, useless wings out as to fly but now only to balance as they sped towards the fence. Long blue-black necks and big eyes constantly astonished at the world as they passed through it.

The leading emu hit the fence with an almost comic intensity. Bounced off it, rebounding, yards back; another one going halfway through the wire, tearing itself to pieces. The dingoes watched as the carnage unfolded.

The wires breaking and another of the emus entangling as the others trampled over it and continued their frantic travel. Bodies moving side to side and up a rise and disappearing over the other side into the eastern desert. Not looking back for an instant, just running, seemingly unaware of the injured birds left behind them. One of the weitj was badly hurt, entangled in the wire and another was sitting, dazed by the collision. Yet another had deep lacerations across its breast, unable to walk. It began calling, grunting and booming in the direction of the running mob.

The young dog leapt forward before she could stop him. Make him understand to check and see what was making the emu run at the fence like they did. To wait. To circle and listen, to get downwind and stay alive. She stood and growl-barked at him and he stopped as if he had hit a wall. Putting his front feet forward and backside down, he skidded to a halt.

An army vehicle came from the direction the emus had come. It drove down an incline and turned onto the track alongside the rabbit-proof fence and stopped near the injured birds.

Two men got out of the vehicle and crossed to the emus. Both carrying rifles, dressed the same in a drab green. Hats with emu feathers in them. The dogs watched as the soldiers aimed their rifles, and shot the three birds. Opened and closed the bolts on their rifles, bright brass flicking out. Shot them again. One took a knife and cut several handfuls of feathers from the dead birds.

A third man, white bearded, had emerged from the vehicle. He was looking in their direction, the shooter with the ruined car. He began limping up the slope to where they were lying. He too was carrying a long rifle. Behind him the soldiers were cutting the left foot off each of the birds. The proof of bounty.

She immediately wheeled away from the hiding place and began sprinting across the ground. The young dog followed her as best he could, bounding along on three legs. They crossed over a small ridge, turned right and ran north, parallel and beneath the crest until it eased down into a scrub-covered gully.

She stopped in the smoke bush and rock heather. Panting, saliva dripping from her tongue, blinking, she lifted her nose, trying to quiet the sounds of her rasping breath. The heaving of lungs. The young red dog was terrified; he trembled and tried to get as close to her as he could. She put her open mouth on his open mouth to stop them both from whining aloud. To save their lives.

No shot came.

They heard the old man shooter speaking to the other men on the ridge. He yelled when he spoke.

The click as he lifted the bolt of the rifle to make it safe.

One of the younger men said something and the old man replied. The three of them turned away and disappeared from the skyline. After a moment the old man reappeared. She heard his howls and maddened words. Threatening sounds and then another's pleading. A fainter voice to cease the howling man.

Clara stopped the Land Rover in a hollow out of sight of the homestead. The voices of the dogs coming down through the jacaranda and lilac trees, through the coral tree and across the sheep yards and gates and fences. They knew she had returned and were struggling to contain themselves. The Land Rover motor was still running and Clara was staring straight ahead, both hands on the steering wheel. Lew looked at her and opened the door, got out and closed the door. Bent to look at her again through the window. 'Your father will be angry. He said it was impossible. When I asked him.'

She turned her face and smiled at him. For a moment her eyes were like a prisoner's and she shook her head. 'No, I'll speak to Dad. I will tell him about us. He will let you stay then.'

She pulled on the handbrake, got out of the vehicle and came around to him. Raised herself on tiptoes, her chin lifted, and put her arms around him. He could feel each of her fingers on his back and it was as if she had found something that was as precious as any treasure. She smelled so cleanly of the cave and the water of the springs. The fine sand and ochre dust of the cave still in her hair.

'No one saw us,' she whispered into his neck. 'But I want them to. I do.'

'I do too,' he said. 'Clara.'

She held his face then for just a moment, let go and walked back around the vehicle and got in. Put the Land Rover into gear, released the handbrake and drove away to the turn-off that led back to the homestead.

Jimmy was standing on the wooden veranda, emptying the teapot into the garden. He saw Clara as she parked the vehicle and walked to the house carrying the woven bags and wet towels.

'Afternoon Miss Clara. You been having a good picnic? Swimming?'

'Afternoon Jimmy.' She smiled and held one hand out into fading sunshine.

'You look happy Miss Clara.'

'Yes, it was lovely thank you,' she said.

'You out for long drive. Good the rain last night isn't it?' Jimmy studied her. 'Right as rain this time. Let's hope.'

Clara nodded, her arms folded. Looked up at the sky. The air cooling in the late afternoon. Biting her bottom lip, smiling and nodding, knew Jimmy had something else to say. 'Yes?'

He stared at her for a while longer before he spoke. Bowed his head in respect. 'Must be very careful but, Miss Clara.'

She looked at him. 'And why is that Jimmy?'

'Must be very careful talking with *puki*. This one. *Puki* got no brains.' Jimmy pointed to his groin and made a sad face. 'Must be very careful? Sorry but I see you take Mr Lew for picnic to Daybreak.'

Clara burst into a laugh, closed her eyes. Shook her head slightly and walked inside. Her arms still folded.

Jimmy flinched as she turned away. 'You want dinner then miss?' he asked. 'Eggs poached like you like. Some bacon crispy. Cup of chocolate I got chocolate. For good daughter of Mr John...*ha ha* strawberry jam. My strawberry. Cumquat too.' He knew how Clara sometimes enjoyed bacon and eggs for her evening meal. Smiled as he heard her call back at him.

'That would be so good, beautiful Mr Jimmy. You are a darling harbour. I am bloody starving.'

Jimmy nodded. 'Don't say bloody Miss Clara.' She had forgiven him.

She had not heard. 'Thank you Mr Jimmy. I love you.'

Oh yes I love you too, he thought. Nodded, unsmiling now. Swimming picnic my arse and sandwiches, ginger beer and boom boom *jimak* all day. Need your strength girl. For that. Darling harbour. My my.

Heard her close her door. She sang something.

You singing now wonder how long you singing, he thought. Bringing home that baby kangaroo Gwen. No wonder you happy ankles saying hello *puki* meet Mr Lew with the smile. Friendly one. Making her want to laugh all the time, he is the boom boom Charlie. Gwen not the only thing he giving her, yes it is, and already speak like him, saying bloody.

Throw her life away with a boy like him, shearer rubbish.

Run away like his father I heard about him too, old Mr Mac a bad bugger. You can tell how she laughing at me. Oh yes I can save a big mess, Mr John he need to know about this one all right no worries.

'Get out here son. You in big trouble.' An angry voice began to wake him.

Lew was lying on his bed, the rolled swag at his feet. He had been dozing. Going in and out of sleep, smiling and half-dreaming of Clara swimming. Suddenly also of Maureen, not having a grave into which to drop a handful of sand for her Peter. Having instead other men's children. The handpiece became a lizard and as he knelt into the long blow along the spine of the sheep he bent its neck back over his knee and stepped, dancing, making the short cross-throat blows to finish shearing this sheep, keeping it alive no matter what. Lifting the hogget's front leg and walking backwards now in a desperate race to fall down the tally-out chute and into the cold water of Daybreak. He dropped the laughing lizard and it buzzed and jumped around at his feet.

'Get out here Lewis McCleod, the young idiot.'

It was Painter's voice calling out to him. He had never heard him so angry. Lew groaned and rolled over, trying to go back to where he had been. Pulled the pillow over his head and drifted.

'I won't tell you again boy. Do I have to come in and get you?'

Lew sat up and stretched. Stood and walked out onto the veranda and looked down. 'What's the problem?' Lew yawned. 'Mate.'

Painter, his hands on his hips. His ropy arms and shoulders were tensed. The tattoos seemed to stand out around him. 'What's the problem with you more like? Got your cock caught in the cash register there son, no worries.'

'Hold on now,' Lew said and walked down the wooden steps to stand opposite Painter.

Painter was furious, yelling at Lew. Veins rising in his arms, in his throat. 'You way way over the line here boy. The boss's daughter. That Clara Drysdale is forbidden territory.'

'What're you sayin'?'

'That Jimmy Wong come runnin' like the big-mouthed laughing cunt he is. Couldn't wait to tell us.'

'Hold on a minute.'

'She don't care about you. Those landowner girls just havin' fun with the croppy boys. They all like the thought of the shearer's cock mate. Ticket of leave ploughboys is what we are. Got no idea what's at stake here. Bond or free, son.' Painter said, shaking his head. 'No idea.'

Lew leaned towards Painter, pointed at him. 'That's enough now. That shit talk.'

Painter stepped back. 'Don't point at me like that,' he said. 'Enough? Fuck son, you got no clue to what enough is.'

'What?'

'I asked him not to come after you.' Painter glanced back

towards the homestead. 'I told him we are gone and won't be back. This Tuesday morning gone. He's paid us, I got the cheque. We have to get going now son.'

'Don't call me son.'

'What?'

'You heard me.'

'Well now. Like that is it?'

'I am going nowhere. I am staying here. With Clara. She'll be having a word with her father. Work it out with him.'

'You don't know what you are saying. He will never work any fucking thing out, with you or his daughter mate.'

'Well,' Lew said, 'you always seem to know so much. You know nothing old man. Jesus, you even hate that Jimmy for just being who he is.'

'Now you hold on a minute.'

'And you sayin' grace before each meal like a clown. Just getting attention I reckon.'

'That's got nothin' to do with this.'

'Or what about your wife? Mary, is it? I didn't even know you had a wife. You left her didn't you? You knock her about when you mad drunk? Your missus? You nasty old bastard.'

'Well well.' Painter took two steps to one side and raised his fists to his waist. Crossed back as if in a boxing ring to touch gloves. Banged his knuckles together. 'Best that is enough now young Mr McCleod.' He began moving from side to side as he spoke, forcing a smile. 'Well well.' He let his bottom lip slip onto his top lip. 'Son.'

'You did, didn't you? Bashed her? Make you feel good when you hurt her?'

Painter hissed, 'Yeah I did, liked it too. Smashed her stupid face in. Laughed as I did it too. Easier cause they weak, see. Women. Throw them against the wall mate. Cunts. Give me a hard-on when they cry. Beg. You so high now you been loved for a bit son?'

Lew did not raise his hands, bit his bottom lip to stop his mouth shaking. It was as if his heart was breaking as he heard the old man speak.

'You just like your mother, boy. Weak. What do you know anyway, still thinking with your cock.'

'I know more than you ever will old man. I love her and I would never hurt her. Not like you, full of hate for anything that shows you tenderness. You evil when you drink.'

Painter was moving constantly, dipping his head and rolling his shoulders. 'Full of hate is it? Think you are a fightin' man now? That woman has made you think you are bold and strong. Look at me. How ugly I am. You got one brain Mr McCleod,' Painter spat on his hands, 'and that's between your legs.' Opened and closed his fingers as he always did before a punching fight. Laughed. 'Fight me boy if you think you can.'

Lew had seen this and knew this is what he did before he fought, say everything, truth and lies to make them angry and you'll win every time but he didn't care and threw himself at the old tattooed man with the don't touch me arms.

'I'm a better man than you'll ever be you ignorant old bastard,' he yelled and ran at him.

Painter sidestepped and watched as Lew ran past. Pretended to kick out at his backside. Acting out something almost slapstick. 'Well you are not a fist fighter, that's for certain. I will hurt you if you keep this up. I might even enjoy it. Not like fucking your mother. She was hopeless. Like you.'

Lew turned, spinning in the dust, and approached Painter. Looked at him. This impossible old man with the broken face. Wanting to love him and beat him down at the same time. Be better than him and his filthy mouth.

Lew swung a wide right hand towards his head. Painter stepped back and bobbed. Came up and hooked Lew in the ear. Followed that with a right to his neck. Another hard left hook, this time into his ribs, stepped away.

'Old man is it? Ignorant? Yes boy, I am the worst old man you will ever meet. A hiding will do you the world of good.'

Lew staggered back, coughed and was struggling to clear his throat. Kept swallowing.

Painter blew out through his nose, made a come here gesture with his fists, banging them together. 'Should have, years ago. Come on then Mr McCleod, knock me down with a feather.'

Lew put his head down and ran straight at him, grabbed him around the waist as Painter punched into his lower back above his kidneys. They held, staggered backwards and crashed into the ground. Dust rose as they rolled over in the dirt. Arms and legs and Lew was first to stand up and recover. He stood over a coughing Painter. Raised his foot, callused heel facing down as if to stab it into his face.

'Righto.' Painter relaxed, lay back and closed his eyes. 'All right, all right mate you win.'

'You finished?'

Painter, looking at the ground, nodded.

Lew stepped away.

They could hear each other's hard breathing.

'Enough,' Lew said, 'you should not have said that stuff. I know that's what you do.'

'You know why?'

'Yep, I know why.'

'Welcome to the world boy, you are your own man now.' Painter rolled over. Coughed, retched and raised himself up. Hands on knees, wheezing as he struggled to catch his breath.

Lew stretched out his hand to help him stand and Painter swivelled. He hit Lew with a rising left hook to his cheek, a straight right to the forehead. Lew's head snapped left and back and then the world became black. Throat closing. Two more punches to the ear and back of the head as he fell.

Painter stepped over him, watching as he put his hands on his hips. 'What did you fucking expect? Son?'

He stood there until he heard the first shotgun blast. His head came up. Another blast and then two more in quick succession. Coming from somewhere near the dog kennels.

King looked away from the old man. He looked to where he could hear her coming for them. He knew her sound and the smell of her. King would not acknowledge the old man as he levelled the shotgun. His tail wagged only for her; even with the terrible fear in her voice, he felt the joy that was her coming for them and lifted his chin. And then her father blew his head off.

Boofy snarled and charged at the old man and he too was shot dead.

John Drysdale broke open the Remington twelve gauge and extracted two spent shells. Tossed them to one side and inserted two fresh cartridges. White smoke curled from the barrels. He snapped the breach shut and shot Jess and Fleet.

Clara screaming as she ran. Her father looked to where she was running across the paddock from the homestead. Flicked the opening lever with his thumb. Again, extracted the spent shells, reloaded. Lifted the gun to his shoulder and shot Swift and Bill. Sky had retreated into her birthing kennel. John kicked it over and shot her in the back of head as she cowered from him. One of the yearling pups had crawled away on its belly to the limit of its chain. Her tail between her legs. John stepped forward and dragged her closer and shot her too.

Clara reached him and pushed him; stood, bent over and panting, her mouth open staring at the slaughter. The bodies of her dogs in the kennel lines. The blood and matter of such familiar coat markings. He had shot each of them in the head so she no longer recognised their faces.

She began screaming at her father.

He recovered from her push, stepped forward and hit her back-handed across the face. Hissed words to her she had never heard him use. She staggered and immediately stopped screaming, opened her mouth and eyes wide, looked at the ground. Silent. Blood coming from her nose.

'I left you her,' her father said, his voice soft now. Pointed with the gun barrels to the bitch Dee who had curled into a ball as if trying to make herself invisible. She was unmoving and terribly still except for spasms of trembling coming through her.

'You only need the one dog, girl,' he said. 'And she is barren so when she dies you will have to buy another. Won't you?' Her father broke the shotgun open and allowed the barrels to point to the ground. 'You always kept far too many dogs young lady.' He turned and walked towards the dressage yards.

Clara fell to her knees and began a dreadful wailing. There were no intelligible words coming from her except please. And, don't Dad.

*

Jimmy was standing on the veranda, a hand shading his face. He was holding a towel in the other hand and watching where the shooting came from. His face contorted, mouth open in horror. He began waving the white teatowel as he realised what was happening.

John Drysdale reached the handling yard.

The shooting and screaming had unsettled the black filly. She was tossing her head and racing around and around the circular yards, her feet throwing up sawdust. She saw him, smelled the blood, stopped and turned away from the old man and cocked her hips as if in warning that she would kick him if he came close. He stepped to one side and shot her in the belly with both barrels.

The blast threw her onto her side and she tried to stand. The pink coils of her intestines had come out of her and she stepped in them. Staggered, gave a high-pitched noise and fell to her front knees. Nose to the ground.

John reloaded. He levelled the shotgun and shot her in the head. 'Good,' he said. He did not like to see an animal suffer unnecessarily. He didn't even know if his daughter had named the young horse yet. Spoke again to himself, language he never used. 'Where's that fucking cunt kangaroo with the straw hat? Gwen is it?'

He did not see Jimmy as he came up behind him. Only heard, 'Sorry Mr John,' as Jimmy hit him over the back of the neck with a length of wood.

Drysdale sprawled forward and Jimmy stepped over him and hit him again, this time on the side of the head above his ear. He kicked the shotgun away and knelt next to the old man. 'Sorry

Mr John but you *gila gila*. Oh my good God Miss Clara I did not know he do this. I am very sorry. He go crazy your father.'

His accent was strong as he took a roll of bandages from his pocket and tied Drysdale's hands behind his back. Rolled him onto his back and looked to where Miss Clara was still kneeling and wailing.

The dingo listened and heard the vehicle start and drive away. The sound of the motor faded and soon there was no sound of them at all. The quiet of the country without the men in it returned. Her breathing slowed.

Her heart too began to slow its beat. She would wait another hour before she emerged from the gully. She had taken her mouth from the young dog's mouth and licked her lips. Licked his mouth and looked at him. His fear and trembling. She crawled out of the deep fold in the land, lay down and waited in the covering at the edge of the scrub. Watched the red male and closed her eyes. Rested her chin on the ground and waited.

He joined her and they lay as still as they could until the dog crows found them. The black feathered demons began hopping and flapping in the bushes above them. Cawing and calling waahdong, their judgment; their mocking of her and her kind. The thought of emerging into the open country from the cover of the blue and smoke bush daunted her but at the same time she knew they would have to move. The damned dog crows were telling the world they were there. The old man with the car and the rifle would soon see these things and return. She rose and ran at the black feathered devils, snapped at them.

Resumed the need to run east and, as she began to trot, she began to see before her images of the man hunting them and how he would know their line of travel; how he would know they had been steadily moving into where the sun rose. East. The need to find water was once again growing and as they ran into more and more strange country the knowledge of places diminished.

His moving car and his arms raised, forming, shooting and disappearing in the ground before her as she ran.

She breasted a ridge and again saw below the long fence and how it stretched right away to the bokadje line where the earth meets sky. The young dog caught up and stopped with her and they lay panting and watching the fence and the darkening land, the sun falling behind them. The crows seemed to have given up for a while and the afternoon sun was coming down over the earth in a wide view for as far as she could see.

She came to a decision to cut through country. She knew of an abandoned township. Water would have gathered there from the storms.

A wide looping backtrack and then they could follow ancient river lines, continue into the interior where no men no cars would follow. Backtrack yet again to return to the line of rocks that was the head of Winjilla Springs. There was the ancient place to den. Fresh water close and rock caves. But first she would mislead.

She stood, wheeled away to her right side and began to trot to the south.

The young red dog, frowning, panting, his injured leg beginning to touch the ground a little, began, as usual and unquestioning, to follow her.

Painter was staring in the direction of the shooting. 'What the hell is going on? Shooting off that shotgun boss? Something's wrong.'

Lew began convulsing and Painter rolled him onto his side. Pulled his rigid arms together and down towards his knees. Took off his Jackie Howe vest and made a rough pillow. He stood up and leaned back down with his hands on his knees as he stared into Lew's swelling face. 'No. No you don't. I believed in you son, don't let me down now.'

Painter straightened, turned his back to look towards the woolshed.

'Fuckin' kid,' he said. 'Didn't even have a pair of shoes when I met you. Still shit'n yellow.'

Thought about the location of his Bible. Next to his bed, on the floor. He could see the shape of the woolshed. And above the corrugated-iron building, surrounded by trees and the sky, a ghost shadow of the coming moon already rising.

He bowed his head. 'The priest O'Donnell, son. Forbid

them not to come unto me: the little children.' He put his thumb up to his nostril, blew snot onto the ground. 'For something something suffer…enter the Kingdom of Heaven. Yeah, that's it.' Some of the snot blew across his ribs and belly and he looked up. 'O'Donnell? Some other cunt maybe.'

An old man, bare chested with muscles like twisted ropes in arms and shoulders and chest. He began walking and shadow boxing. Shuffling feet, bobbing and ducking his head. Once he slapped both hands onto his chest. Across his back an entire crucifixion scene.

More shotgun blasts, and then more. He looked again to where they were coming from and then he heard a woman. It was young Clara and she was screaming.

His eyes became wide and he began to run towards the screaming. Calling out.

'Hold on, hold on.'

It had been a week. Perhaps ten days. Following the outlines of a raised gravel road, Lew had driven John Drysdale's Series I Land Rover due east for two hours. He stopped at a crossroads with a rock cairn, a black metal pole and signposts. Daybreak Springs 15 miles, pointing from where he had come; beneath that: Thompsons Find 5 miles.

He switched off the engine and did not move as he thought about the last week.

A night, a day and a night again till he woke. He didn't know how long it had been. It had hurt when he breathed and it hurt when he tried to walk. His urine red with blood.

Jimmy had said to him, Mr John he is not well no. He was standing at the front door of the homestead.

Painter had gone too but was true to his word and had sent the doctor who drove out from Gungurra that same day. Dr Fraser had wanted to move Drysdale to a Perth hospital but Jimmy said, no, Mr John he don't want to go. Lew remembered the doctor examining him. Saying he had concussion but there was nothing broken apart from his nose. His fingers on the grating ribs. Confirming that they were cracked but otherwise he was all right internally apart from bruised kidneys. Spleen good. Liver fine. The doctor bandaged and strapped his ribs; kept the strapping in place with two diagonal shoulder bandages.

'Where is the daughter?' Dr Fraser asked as he worked. 'Clara, is it?'

Jimmy watching them. 'She out riding doctor, be gone all day. It's hard on her y'know. She not herself anyway after mother.'

'What's been going on out here?' the doctor said. 'Mr Drysdale has had, well, there's the stroke of course. But what are these blows to his head?' He took off his glasses to look at them both.

Jimmy stepped forward. 'When Mr John fall down he roll around, hit his head. Mr Lew fall off horse before, very bad luck same time and Mr John it just happen too. Isn't it. Maybe he get big fright from Mr Lew falling.' Jimmy speaking in feigned stupidity and innocence. 'Ask Mr Lew if you want.'

'Is that right Lewis?' the doctor asked, staring at him. 'I may have to call in to the police station about this.'

'You don't have to. Just bad luck. All at the same time, Doc. Just happened mate.' Lew said and tried to smile through his bruised face.

'Yes. I see.'

The doctor left Jimmy with a bottle of pills and instructions to bring Mr Drysdale into the Gungurra hospital if his condition deteriorated. Said the next one might kill him.

Jimmy nodding and thanking the doctor.

Lew saw old man Drysdale sitting at the end of the veranda.

He had not been shaved and saliva bubbled from a corner of his mouth. The stubble on his chin and throat as white as smoke bush. His neck hung in loose wattles and his burnt face shining red. His damaged eye was closed; fluid streamed almost constantly. He was holding a handkerchief to his face with his right hand. Food stains on his shirt and trousers. His left hand like a rubber glove, useless and livid. Held at an awkward angle in front of his groin.

Drysdale, trying to say something but seeming instead to be yawning, hissed, winked and turned away. He reached out with the hand holding the handkerchief, waving it at Lew. Making angry noises. His head sagged and he appeared to weep.

'You fucking old bastard,' Lew said softly. 'What you did, you selfish fucking old bastard.'

Jimmy was calling out from somewhere in the house. 'Mr John where are you? You hiding from me. Time for your tablets isn't it.' His laughter.

When Jimmy came, he was holding two white tablets in the palm of his hand and a glass of water with two straws. A towel over his shoulder. He stopped and stared at Lew. 'You better go Mr Lew, upsetting Mr John. I mean it,' he said and was not laughing or smiling. 'I mean it OK?'

'Where is Clara, Jimmy?' Lew asked. 'I want to see her.'

Jimmy giving him a hard look.

'She no come out room, Mr Lew. Best you stay away for while. She not speaking to anybody even to me. Best you go away now. Please Mr Lew.'

By the time the dingo bitch smelled young goats on the wind her hunger had become constant.

They had come up to the old township from the west and were safely downwind of the herd of goats the old man kept. Her mother's hunting, the beginning of her knowledge of the world. All the animals of the old men to be approached with much caution but the reward was usually an easy kill. She waited for the young dog to catch up to her. They heard singing coming from the stone house with the series of offset walls and gardens spaced out towards the east. She knew there was water there; drinking troughs for the goats. The smell of it coming on the wind.

The old man emerged from the stone house and the young dingo's tail immediately shot between his legs. He whimpered and put his head onto the sand and began to backtrack. It was the old bearded man with the car. The shooter who had slaughtered his clan. Almost killed them.

He looked at the bitch in confusion. She too was lying flat on the sand, but she was studying the movements of the old man. Saliva dripped from her tongue and lips and once again the unceasing hunger made the whole world alive to her. She almost whined but instead opened and closed her mouth and continued to pant. Would never be so weak to her hunger as to become vulnerable. Again the schooling of her mother and grandmother, the awareness in her body. What good to the whelp, the pack, dead? Be hungry, eat, after the kill. Above them the sun rose and the day was hot.

The young red dog crawled forward, touched her nose, licked as if to bring her to her senses, to run away from this madness. Her hackles rose, a low growl from her throat.

They waited until nightfall. Lights came from the windows of the house and then they heard a great crash and silence. After a while, the old man began shouting and there was solitary laughter. Singing.

She walked backwards, turned and trotted north into the old town cemetery until she found an urn filled with stormwater from the rains. Drank. The night was closing on them and she waited until she heard the sound of sweet frogs alongside a brush-filled line of abandoned and sunken gravesites. The rain had brought them. They sang in their pleasure, like morning sun on a cold body.

The young red dog was a few paces back, lying on the day warmth of a stone and cement slab. He watched as she pounced and took a frog. Lifted it slightly, threw it up and swallowed it whole. Gulped, paused, looked at him to say this is how it is done, now you eat. Hunt, you young fool. He walked over the brush hollow which had become silent and waited, shooting glances at her as she returned to the funeral urn and again began to drink, lapping the water.

He made several unsuccessful leaps into the croaking frog hollow. Stood, staring at her with a crinkly mouth. She turned and trotted away from him into the old processing area of rusting iron tanks and bricks and broken buildings.

He looked at the Daybreak Springs, Thompson's Find signpost again, opened the door of the Land Rover, stepped out and closed the door.

The silence of the land seemed to make the noise of the closing door longer. He stretched his hands above his head. His ribs hurt. Bent to touch his feet to ease his back muscles. Only made it to his knees.

His eyes were still yellow-bruised, his mouth scabbed from where Painter had beaten him, but his face and head had stopped aching. He touched his cheekbone with his fingers and felt his broken lips. Cleared his throat. He did not believe Painter would have done that to him until he did. He walked around to the passenger's side and urinated into a ditch. Spat also. The blood had gone from his water.

He got back into the Land Rover, started the engine and drove towards Thompson's Find. The track was potholed and corrugated. Thought about the day Painter left.

*

The morning had been hot. The sun overhead in the blue sky. Painter packed his swag, checked the oil and water in the truck. Filled up the tank from the forty-four-gallon drum of petrol on the back tray. Wearing his old brown moleskin pants and shearers vest, the Traveller hat pushed back on his head and still those don't touch me arms. Hands like broken feet, he would say.

He came to where Lew was standing. The air was still, a sudden screech of galahs and far away the bleating of sheep. Crows protesting. Painter nodded.

'The boss is fucked. Jimmy got him flush on the uncle with that stick. Twice. Didn't think the cunt had it in him.'

'And Clara?'

'At least the old bastard didn't shoot her. She'll be right.'

Painter was holding out his hand. Lew couldn't see his face properly; it swam before his eyes. Rain on the windscreen. He took the old man's hand and shook it.

They stood there for a minute.

'Yep.' Painter said and got in behind the wheel.

'You know how to drive?' Lew asked.

'I know how to drive. Hard part is convincing the wallopers I didn't bloody steal it.' Big smile. No teeth.

Lew stepped away from the truck and watched as Painter drove down the red gravel track towards the Great Eastern Highway. The truck got smaller and smaller. Brackets of red dust coming together and turning into spirals above the cab in the heat, the engine whine climbing. Change bloody gears, Painter. Go on now.

Painter changed up and Lew watched until the truck disappeared. He would never have said sorry.

*

When Lew reached the outskirts of Thompson's Find, he passed the cemetery. Ornate railings surrounded the white marble headstones. Black writing. A mournful white angel with a raised index finger. Rows of metal and marble crosses, headstones, beds of white quartz. Walkways between graves wide enough for four men to carry coffins. A myrtle bush thriving against a monument of red bricks. Grey, termite-ravaged fence posts leaned north-south; red wires sagged, holding them in place. A painted wrought-iron gate had been left open and was off its top hinge. He changed gears and slowed the Land Rover further. Leaned the underside of his forearms and wrists on the steering wheel and studied the ruins of the town as he drove into it.

An ugly pair of stunted, hopelessly foreign-looking oak trees partly obscured the outline of a crumbling stone church. A granite cross made from local stone remained on the apex. Beneath the cross, an empty window space in a perfect circle, the stained glass of the rose long gone. Collapsed and scorched roof timbers, two beams like fingers pointing in a defiant gesture towards the sky. The English trees should have died a long time ago. Perhaps they had. One was orange. The other a sickly grey.

The feral cat was ginger striped and had beautiful yellow eyes. In its mouth the throat of a honeyeater it had taken. The broken wings askew.

The young dingo saw her first and raced into the granite heather to attack.

The cat transformed, suddenly becoming a crazed explosion of fur and claws. Seemingly larger now, backing off yet hissing and spitting at the dog in open-mouthed fury, left and right paws slashing.

The boy dingo stood his ground at first, growling and showing his teeth. Lowering his head to snarl and watch. The cat yowled, hissed again and launched into a counterattack, running straight at him as if sensing his inexperience. He retreated, yelping, running away and looking back into the scrub with horror. Claw marks down his forehead and across his snout; spots of blood. His tail pressed once again between his legs.

The bitch glanced at him and immediately leapt into the bushes. The orange demon flew to attack her but she simply snarled and lunged into the savagery; took the cat by the head and snapped it like a snake, smashing its body back and forth onto the ground.

She let the body drop from her mouth and placed a paw on its neck. Using her front teeth, she opened the cat's belly and exposed the bodies of five or so fledglings, baby zebra finches. She ate the half-digested birds and ripped the cat apart further to get to the liver and heart. Ate them also and turned back to the sulking youngster. Stared at him for a while and moved away from the cat's body.

The young dog edged forward. He had seen how she took the cat. He nosed at the bloody carcass and after a few more tentative sniffs and licks he too began to feed.

On the eastern edge of Thompson's Find there was a long copse of blackened mooja and gimlet trees. Behind them, a metal tower with portholes cut at regular lengths. Three wooden poles with wire strung between them. A large rusting cyanide tank with lines of rivets around its girth and up one side. The flotation plant alongside the tank. It was shaped like an enormous funnel and held in place with bolted angle-iron supports.

A corrugated-iron roof had collapsed onto the ground and fallen to one side. Two large rusting wheels with metal poles through their axles. More sheets of corrugated iron at awkward angles in the ruin. The site was covered in the rubble of bricks and masonry. A dead thorn tree wrapped with galvanised metal piping.

Lew continued into the main street of the town. He passed a set of stockyards and what was left of a Bickford aerated bottling plant. A twenty-head stamper and steam boiler lay rusting and abandoned beside the road. It still bore the metal imprint

Ferguson and Sons Engineering Ltd Glasgow above the coal door. A burnt-out blacksmiths and livery stable. The wrought-iron sign still on the gates above the entrance: McGillivray's Blacksmith's and Iron Works.

The first large building he came to was a newspaper office. Thompson's Find *Enquirer* 1900 painted on the façade. Yellow and black paint peeling and the stonework was showing through. An ancient press, left at the front of the building. Its brown rust embossed David Payne and Co. Ltd on one brace; above that: Makers Ottley. Wharfedale. Frozen wheels, rusted fast, rollers and a large flywheel with ratchet teeth. A wooden support frame and wire basket.

Directly opposite, another crumbling Edwardian facade. Collapsed verandas and tall windows. The Good Intent Hotel. The sign had slipped ninety degrees so that it had to be read on the vertical. The L of hotel was at the top and the G of good was at the bottom. He turned his head as he read and passed on.

He rounded a corner slowly, and standing in the middle of the street was an old man. He had a large white beard and was wearing stained canvas trousers, an old fashioned collarless shirt buttoned to his throat, no tie and a sleeveless vest. A large belled-out hat with a snakeskin band.

Behind him, four black and tan horned goats in harness. The cart, resembling a cut-down trap, was piled high with sandal-wood branches. This precious load was secured with ropes tied off with sheepshank knots, pegs of wood through the loops.

The old man waited as Lew stopped the vehicle, got out, closed the door and walked to him.

'Gidday mate.'

'Smith,' the old man said. 'Abraham Smith.' He offered his hand.

Lew nodded to the old man and shook his hand. 'My name is Lewis McCleod, Mr Smith. How are you?'

'I am well. Yourself?'

'You the dingo shooter been down Drysdale Downs and Yate Valley Station? John Drysdale mentioned us to you I believe.'

'I was.'

'I got some bad news about Mr Drysdale,' Lew said, 'he's had a stroke. Being cared for by Jimmy Wong, the cook.'

The old man stared at him. 'Sorry to hear that,' he said. 'Been bad luck around that place, Drysdale Downs. Lost Mrs Drysdale last year I think.'

'That's right.'

Other buildings, the Miners Institute and Post and Telegraph Office. Alongside that a Share Trading and Loans office and further down again, a smaller building. Berwick Moreing Mine Management and Engineering.

'I knew John's father, William Drysdale. Knew him as Bill,' Abraham said. 'Helped him clean up the show around Winjilla just after the war, y'know.'

'I heard that.'

'Killed on the station…when? Some years now. Looking for gold, the old fool.'

'I have heard that.'

'There is a daughter?'

'Yes.' Lew looked away.

Off to one side on some flat ground running out towards the mines, the football oval. One set of goalposts remained and some spectator seating ran around the oval. Cement posts with wooden planks. A small covered stand with central stairs and filigree balustrades. A scoreboard: Visitors 1 6 12 and below that Thompson's Tigers 16 18 114.

'Never leaves you, that foolishness,' Abraham said.

'Did you get that dingo bitch?' Lew asked. 'The one that came back to the Downs woolshed and took a hogget?'

'She runnin' with a young red male? Come up out of the Yate Valley? I tracked her for Drysdale. Told him the story.'

'He said.'

'Well.' Abraham waited a moment and looked back at his goats. 'If it's the one I saw, she is smart as any lubra. Never seen the like come to think of it. Wrecked my old Vauxhall chasin' them I did. She in pup and must be getting ready soon.'

'Could you tell me where she's most likely to be? I want to get some of those dingo pups. Raise them up.'

'That right?'

'Yep.'

'Well you will wish you didn't once you do. Dingos, you see what they do to a birthing ewe? The lambs?'

'No,' Lew shook his head.

The old man blinked and put his chin up. 'No good. Eat a lamb right out of the mother as it's being born. I come,' he clicked his front teeth together and hissed. 'They gone. Best just clean 'em up.'

'Can you raise them to change, Mr Smith?'

'No young fella that's their nature. Best to destroy them.'

The street ran to a long view of rising ground and hillocks where the mines were located. Derelict poppet heads, small volcano shapes of grey tailings and yellow waste rock. Broken and sagging sets of rail lines running to the top of the slag heaps. Rusting orange storage tanks and a single tall red brick smoke stack. Engine houses around the head frames. Ruined workers cottages in rows leading up to the mine gates. A narrow road curving between the cottages.

'Why'd you stop with that bitch? She get away?'

The old man raised a hand and rubbed it across his eyes and face. 'She took that young red with her from Yate Valley Station and got away all right. I went out with those army boys on contract to cull the emus…Got the horrors, come back,' he said. 'Time before that I tore the guts out of my car. Did I tell you?'

One of the goats bleated and Abraham turned to it and raised a stick. Hushed it.

Lew nodded. 'Got the what came back?' he asked.

'Bad dreams. The horrors, from the war. The first one. Like a black stone in my guts and in behind my eyes a giant snake squeezing inside my head. Can't sleep. Can't hunt. What the hell you want dingo pups for?'

Lew shook his head. 'I just do.'

'Well, I don't know if I'll shoot another. She and the young red been here all right. But they doubled back by the look of the tracks. Can you believe it?'

The old man turned and looked at his goats. 'Stay there Eunice,' he said.

Lew looked at him.

'My head nanny, lead goat I always called her Eunice.'

It seemed like a lifetime ago, joking with Painter about this old man dancing with a goat called Eunice, and less funny now.

He wanted to ask why the man would call every goat Eunice, and knew he never would.

Abraham had walked off about ten feet. He knelt. 'Look at these boy. Those dogs been all over here.' He reached out and touched a line of dingo tracks. 'They got four toes and the back pad like a big dog. See the claw marks?' He mused for a while reading the sign. 'There,' he said, 'you see where she heavier on the rear pads, leaning back a little as she run? Carrying her weight over her hips, a sure sign.' He pointed a few feet in front. 'And further on when she lie down, her tits starting to hang. In pup. See where she make water? If you get it fresh you can smell it. That male dog he stronger but an in-pup bitch she strong too. The shape they make when they piss is different. The bitch is oval when they squat. The male they piss in a line, against things if they can and it drips back. Different pattern.'

He pointed to another set of tracks, smaller and rounded. 'They the feral cats,' Abraham looked up and away into the middle distance. 'Gone wild from the people used to live here. Lot of cats round here. Not too many birds.'

Lew knelt next to the old man. He smelled him. Wood smoke and rank fat, an unwashed smell. He reached out and gently touched the tracks as Abraham was doing.

'You don't see the claws with the cat,' Abraham said. 'Retractable see, the cats'. Dingo, like a dog.'

Abraham bent and brushed his hand over a bare piece of earth. He used his finger and the knuckles of his hand to mark out a paw print. Thumbnail marking the edges. 'Fox, same to the dingo except they neater and smaller. Not so heavy. Don't see the fox much when the dingo about. They kill them too. Same as any wild cat they come across.'

The old man pointed back to the original dingo track. 'You can see how long since they been here by which side of the track has had the wind over it. East wind comes in at the daybreak. West at sunset. They been here at least a night ago I would guess. That young red dog has been carrying his back leg where I shot him. See that?'

Lew looked at the line of tracks and saw how the spoor on the left, the near side of the bitch's tracks, had only three heavy and one lighter imprint.

'He is healing though,' Abraham said. 'That bitch must've mothered him up good. I never seen a smarter female all the time I been trackin' them.' Abraham raised up and pointed to another shape about six feet away. Detritus from a ruined building was scattered about, broken timbers, pipes and old solid bricks. 'And there,' he said, 'that'll be their dinner last night.'

Lew looked at the wide recurring S shape with sand pushed up on the lower sides of its travel. Two or three sheets of corrugated iron on the ground.

'Python I would say,' Abraham said. 'Maybe a children's and she been hunting him. That snake be in her belly now I would wager. If I was a betting man.'

She stopped, one paw raised in mid-stride as a python came out beneath a sheet of corrugated iron for an early night hunt. The snake had not seen her and came big-eyed and dappled wet, beautiful into the night. Sweet food white-bellied slithering along towards her. Flickering tongue tasting the air upwind. The ecstasy of snake's muscled coat. Gunya.

It was an easy kill. She took it behind the head. Its body coiling and uncoiling as she crunched it dead. The python hanging from her mouth, she ran to the shelter of a collapsed veranda and shared the hunt with the red dog.

When they had eaten, the bitch took them back to within sight of the old man's house, downwind. They lay hidden in the thin covering of scrub and watched and listened. The smell of the goats and the man came in the air to them, almost something to drink. She heard metal moving in the wind. The bleating of goats in the last of the daylight; how they moved and she watched the kids. The head female had a bell around her neck and as she walked the bell clanked. The dingo saw she had a full udder and that there would be newborn close.

Occasionally the old man would come outside to collect wood. Once he sat and milked one of the goats. She watched him as he moved about. He was a careful man and would stand still and cock his head to one side, listen and wait, studying the land around his house, his eyes going over each detail. Occasionally the young dog would glance at her, lay his chin back down on his paws. He had at last been taught what it was to wait.

The sun was overhead when the wind swung around and their scent carried to the herd. The belled nanny became uneasy and watched where the dog smell was. Her two kids ran and knelt, pushing her back legs apart as they suckled. She stepped over them, the metal bell clanked and she began to walk. Paced the perimeter of the enclosure. Her neck craning, eyes searching the outlying country, the brush and scattered debris of the old town. All the time, the clanking of the metal bell around her neck, keeping time to her pacing.

The dingo, staying on her belly, crawled backwards and rose to a half crouch, swung around to lope away and cross over the leap of the direction of the wind. She knew she could not be seen from behind the old brick walls and the twisted waves of burnt and buckled corrugated iron. It was simply their smell which gave them away, and of course the damned dog crows that continued to plague them.

They trotted back towards the town. Passed across a tennis court and ran into the fallen burnt timbers and iron of a collapsed stand. Ran along the shadowed side of the main street. She sniffed the tyre tracks and footprints. Loose dust blew through the streets, wrapping around poles and the broken facades of the buildings.

She jumped sideways, taking fright at a sudden crash of something falling. Ran in a leap to a side alley. Studied the man's footprints in the sand, the goats' spoor, their pellets, the line of wheel marks. She bent and sniffed at them. They had been here before her and not that long before. She squatted and pissed on their footprints. Looked back at the red dog that had almost begun to put weight on his shot leg.

She lifted her head as she heard, from a long way off, the approach of a vehicle. Yipped at the red dog to listen and they trotted out the side streets of the town into open country. She quickly decided to circle back to the goat yards. Once again, this time upwind, and see if there was a possibility.

They waited in the karrik bush and watched.

Abraham's house was built with the rocks he had gathered. He had cemented them using a burnt lime mix. It was roofed with tiles and had been added to what looked like an old shopfront. He had also built a series of staggered rock walls against the prevailing easterly winds.

Lew watched as the old man removed the harness from the goats and allowed them into a fenced enclosure. He took the piles of sandalwood from the small trap and stacked them on sheets of corrugated iron. Lew lent him a hand and Abraham seemed to appreciate it. When they had stacked the last of the sandalwood, Abraham roofed it with another two sheets of corrugated iron and weighed them down with four bricks. Lew remembered the piles of wood he and Painter had stored away for the next charcoal burn.

'Thank you young fella,' Abraham said. 'Lew McCleod is it?'

'It is.'

'Good good. Come in.'

Lew followed Abraham into his house.

'Your father, they call him Mac? Mac McCleod? A shearer too?'

'Never knew him Mr Smith.'

The old man studied him. 'Abe. You can call me Abe. Sit down, I'll make us some tea.'

Lew sat at a long table topped with thick wooden planks.

Abraham bent to push some sticks into an outdoor oven. It had a square corrugated-iron chimney, a parallel flue used for smoking meat. A back leg, flank and shoulder of a young goat cured dark brown was hanging there behind wire mesh and hessian. When the sticks in the oven caught he added some larger blocks of wood and soon he had a kettle boiling.

'So you going to catch up with those dogs and take the pups?' Abraham sat and poured tea into two tin cups. Added a touch of yellow milk to his cup and spooned in sugar.

Lew lifted the cup to his mouth and blew on the tea. 'I plan to.'

Abraham made a noise of appreciation as he sipped his tea, stirred it and tapped the spoon against the edge of the cup. 'I been hunting dingos for thirty years more or less. Fossicking for gold and picking up sandalwood except when the horrors come. I can't do a damn thing when that's on me, no I cannot.'

Lew held his hands on each side of the cup, watched the steam as it rose.

Abraham looked at him. 'You shear with Painter Hayes?'

'I did.'

'You the young fella he took a shine to. I heard about you. Good shearer they say. Two fifty a day and clean, day in day out. You and old man Painter always running together. Now you by yourself here?'

'I am.'

Abraham frowned, tapped the table. Touched two fingers to his cheekbone. 'He do that to you?'

'No,' Lew said. 'I fell off a horse.'

Abraham looked down at his cup, nodded. 'How many times you fall off that horse boy? Three, four times? Same horse?'

'More like five or six times. Same horse.'

Abraham laughed. 'You all right boy. By God that Painter can fight like a thrashing machine can't he? Never known him to be beaten and when he on the drink, Jesus look out take cover. I saw him once in Derby fightin' the publican and two coppers. Mad drunk he was.'

Abraham stopped laughing and looked at the table, tapped his fingers on the wood. 'Five or six times,' he said and nodded. Repeated to himself in approval of something he did not understand.

Lew cleared his throat. 'Where do you think she has gone to?'

'The dingo bitch?' Abraham looked up. 'Well I believe, like I showed you, she circled back here. Those tracks from last night tell the story.'

Lew nodded as the old man continued to speak.

'I would say she and that young dog have run east into the Sandy. But,' he paused and sipped his tea, 'she will loop twice north and then southwest and come back to her ground. Where she knows best. I believe she will whelp at Winjilla. Her kind been doin' it for a thousand years. Along those lines anyway. Good water, plenty of game and dry rock caves there. The run into the big Sandy is a ruse to fool any following, me that is.

I don't know if she even knows how good she is; by God she is clever. But those pups is close. That Winjilla. Known as Daybreak Springs now.'

'Daybreak Springs?' Lew wanted to laugh.

'Yep, you know it?'

Lew stood up. 'I know it,' he said. 'But it is fenced off.'

'It is fenced off, about two miles of it anyway but she will soon go around it or dig under the wire. Or get the youngster to. You going to shoot them?'

Lew nodded.

'What you got?'

'A shotgun. Twelve gauge. Remington side-by-side.'

Abraham nodded. 'Do the job if you get close enough.'

He stood up and walked inside the house. After a few minutes he returned with a rifle. He laid it on the table. The bolt was open. Placed a spare magazine and a brown box of shells next to the rifle. 'This,' he said, 'is the old fully wooded Lee Enfield .303 Mark Three. It is reliable and accurate. The barrel is stabilised hot and cold by the wood, see. Take it.'

'I have the shotgun,' Lew said.

Abraham touched the stock of the rifle with a finger. 'The shotgun is all right if you are close. This,' he tapped the stock, 'will do the job at two, three hundred yards. Aim at the biggest part of the animal behind the front shoulder. Takes out the heart and lungs, see. Dead before they hit the ground.' He mused for a moment. 'Don't aim at the head.'

Lew picked up the Lee Enfield. He pressed the magazine release, closed and opened the bolt.

'You used one before by the look,' Abraham said.

Lew nodded. 'Was shown.'

'Well, you take it, I have another. That used to belong to old man Drysdale anyway. Get it back to me when you can.'

Lew reached out and shook his hand. 'Thank you,' he said. 'I appreciate this.'

Abraham waited. He looked at Lew and Lew saw a tightening of his mouth. Something uncertain pass across his face. 'Would you do something for me?'

'I will if I can.'

'I have left set traps around Daybreak. And some poison baits. When the horrors came I didn't get back to them. Especially the traps. Would you check them for me please?'

Lew nodded.

He saw Abraham's eyes become frightened as he rubbed a hand across his face. 'I cannot abide,' he said and his voice shook. 'I cannot abide the thought.'

Clara sat on her bed and stared at the door. Was there a stranger behind it? Had someone come to stand between her and the world? Was her mother waiting for her on the other side? Her dogs? She felt cold and when she touched her face with her stiff fingertips it was numb. Her cycle was due and had not come and she did not know why except perhaps that it was all that blood, the dogs and the filly whose name was to be Rain because she had never known the rain except that once, the night before her father came. How could he and why won't it come?

She still wore the moleskins, stiff with the blood of the dogs. She had not changed her clothing. The blood made monstrous patterns on her white shirt. She had not eaten and the blanket had fallen behind her. When night came she simply fell sideways on the bed and looked at the door until she slept.

Lewis was gone and she held his voice to her, I will be back Clara. She clenched her hands into fists around the words that came through the walls and window to her. The memory of his voice was fine and rounded like a river stone smooth like skin and soft and hard and wet…Him at Daybreak Springs and would he bring himself? Where was Gwen? Daddy had become a monster when he stormed in through that door and began shouting at her, have you been with him, is it true? Standing right there with that very door open and yelling no until the saliva rolled out his mouth and he turned and then soon enough after that the shooting started. Nothing making sense.

Jimmy hiding the baby roo in a broom cupboard and Mr Painter Hayes came running, holding her and yelling at Jimmy to get a blanket and take her in the house. Hush now Miss Clara, saying this as Jimmy with his arm around her took her in. She had wet her pants, she remembered this too. And Mr Hayes saying it's all right, doesn't matter. It's nothing.

Then she remembered carrying the dogs to the pit Mr Hayes had dug. Him sweating and being so very kind to her, saying it's all right Miss Clara. It will be all right. Everything passes. Even this and apologising for his mouth. And wanting teeth, the old man gentle with the deaths for her. She said nothing but did not smile at him. No. She said goodbye King and Swift. Oh Boofy you idiot. She could not say all their names aloud but in her mind she did and knew they would know. Saw each of their faces looking at her in adoration. Running with their love behind her, they would have run themselves to death for her. But of course she would never let that happen.

Her father shot them. He shot them into pulp.

She felt a wetness between her legs, pushed her fingers into her pants, looked at the blood. How her mother would have kissed her head with these bloody fingers, say that's all right isn't it and whisper, *Zorro est arrivé*. Her joking code for the arrival of their menstrual cycle. Her voice. 'Zorro came in through the window during the night darling, with his sword in one hand and the curtains in the other. The hero arrives and now there is blood everywhere.' *Zorro est arrivé*. The hilarity of that. The immense toughness of that.

And then she began to sob. She did not think she would ever stop.

The dingo watched from the cover of the brush as the old man began to cross to the goat pen. His legs winding as he sang to the sky and staggered in a wide loop to catch the nanny with the bell around its neck. Dragged her out of the pen and began to dance about with her. Continued to sing, Abide With Me, as the goat tried to pull her feet away from the old man. Sung this a thousand times in Belgium, know the fuckin' words off by heart Eunice. The bell around her neck clanked and her udder was flopping about between her back legs. For the boys. Abide with me fast falls the eventide, the darkness deepens. Off by heart, the words, the boys.

The young red dingo stared and blinked, opened his mouth and began to pant; he too had cried and despaired as he looked out at the havoc of the yate trees. They both turned away.

When the two dingoes left the outskirts of the abandoned town and the house of the old man, the bitch felt the heaviness of her belly. It was the first time since she had known she was carrying the black dog's whelp that she was slowed by them.

Almost milk come on and she was when she cleaned herself, coming on, the knowledge pressing. She knew she would soon have to find a safe den; somewhere near water and away from men who would shoot her. She lay down and waited in the mulga scrub of a gully they were crossing. The young red dog's leg was strong enough now to carry most of his weight and he had run ahead.

He stopped when he noticed her absence and ran back looking for her. He had smelled the smoke, the fire in the scrub. Saw the rising white and grey smoke boiling ahead of the flames, coming through the grass as fast as he could run and he had no idea what to do.

The bitch was lying in some shaded sand, her back legs pushed out by the growing bulk of her belly; her teats were beginning to swell and they itched. The young dog stood and yawped at her. The bitch rose and watched with astonishment as he spun around and began to sprint ahead of the encroaching flames, looking at her to follow him. The smoke was thickening and she could feel the heat, the cracking and hissing sounds as the scrub began to catch and burst. The fire came into the eastern end of the small gully and began to roar as it came up towards her. She knew as her mothers had shown her what to do and immediately ran until she saw a thinning in the flames. Turned and ran directly into it.

In a moment she was through the fire front and was loping across the black burnt-clear ground, the earth hot beneath her feet. She began to increase her speed until she found a hollow where the fire had passed over. Stopped there and waited.

Then she heard the red pup's dismal howling. Dirging at his

loss of her. She listened and crossed back through the swirling grass smoke to where he was. Somehow he had survived, but his whiskers were burnt off and his fur was charred. He looked even more stupid without whiskers. The charred fur on his body and cat-scratched face.

She ran to him, licked his face and he glanced at her and continued to howl. It was as if he would not believe she was really there. She nudged and licked him again. Put her mouth over his head to shut him up. Aware, always aware of other men, other cars. The rifles in their hands.

As Lew drove back towards Drysdale Downs he knew there was nothing to do but follow Abraham's advice. To know and wait where she would return to. Best place to find and kill her.

In just over two hours he saw the outcrop of shining red boulders that marked the turn-off to Daybreak Springs. He drove to the south and found a gully in which to park the Land Rover. Taking the rifle, he walked back to the fence boundary. He came across the rotting body of a wombat and several traps that had been tripped. Came across three more traps still set.

'Jesus,' he whispered, sprang them and kept walking. He found yet another unsprung trap and pushed a stick on the footplate. This trap shut with a savage snap, breaking the stick. Lew looked for the poison baits but they had all gone. Eaten or washed away in the rainstorm. He thought about old man Smith showing him the tracks in the sand. How the horrors made his hands shake.

He opened the gates, left them open and cut around to the

south and climbed a small ridge rising up to some flat boulder-strewn ground. He found what appeared to be the highest point of the surrounding area above the springs themselves. Checked the position of the sun and looked at the time. He went about clearing the area and using fallen scrub to camouflage his position. As he finished, he took note of the wind direction and, again, the time. Where the sun was in the sky. The shadows of the trees and where she would come, if she came. He then backed out to the gates and used a branch to cover his tracks. Within a day and a night, the wind would erase any evidence of his being here.

He took the road to Drysdale Downs knowing he would have to return to Daybreak within the week. The bitch should have whelped by then. Coming to the fork indicating the homestead to the left and woolshed and shearers quarters to the right, he thought for a moment how things had changed. He took the left-hand track and drove up to the front of the homestead.

Jimmy was sitting with John Drysdale on the front veranda, leaning forward with a spoon. He glanced at Lew, nodded to the old man before him and opened his mouth in an encouraging manner, the way a mother would feed a baby in a high chair. Lew could not hear what he was saying but he noticed John had a white napkin around his neck and was opening his mouth in response to Jimmy.

Lew looked away as Jimmy quickly spooned in some mashed potatoes and gravy. Wiped under the old man's bottom lip with the spoon and nodded towards him. 'Good boy.'

Lew opened the door of the vehicle, got out and closed the

door. He saw old man John turn his head slowly to look at him. Still with his mouth open.

'Mr John,' Jimmy said, set the spoon down and stood. He raised his hand towards Lew. 'Mr Lew,' he said and walked down to him.

'Jimmy,' Lew said. 'How's Clara?'

Jimmy looked back at the house and Lew saw her face behind her window. She smiled and raised a hand. Then the curtain fell back.

'She still getting over it.'

'I should go to her,' Lew took a step towards the house.

Jimmy stepped in front of him. 'Please Mr Lew, not now. Please. Too early too early.' His eyes were downcast but he stood his ground.

Lew felt his eyes harden as he looked at Jimmy standing before him. He closed his hands into fists. 'Jimmy.'

'Soon Mr Lew, but I have something to tell you first isn't it? I'm sorry.'

Lew nodding. He flicked a glance towards the veranda. 'And him?'

'No good Mr Lew.' Jimmy hesitated. 'Like baby.'

Lew nodded. He took no pleasure in this.

'But, I have also other things…news so sorry Mr Lew.'

'What?'

'Mr Painter is in hospital.'

'Hospital?'

'He go crazy too, *ayo*, *gila* in Gungurra, fight fight in the pub and fall down after. Big to-do, they all say, he almost died, sorry but it was him most probably.'

'Painter?' Lew leaned forward as he asked. 'You sure?'

'I am sure. Very sick for a while now, Mr Painter. Coughing all the time. You no hear him?'

'No,' Lew said, turned and walked away. He felt his mouth opening and no more words coming out. He did not seem to know how to close it for a while.

The terrible heaviness in her belly decided her. That urgent imperative and for some unknown reason the smell of the sky. Perhaps it was the remembered insistence of her mother to be certain. Become the silence of waiting and the knowing that will come back to you. Little pieces of who you are will join, like a heart beating. Like the blood from a wound. A wild dog does not think such things.

The wind had come and it was full of the growing foul stink of the white men from the west country. It was heavy and coming from where the sun set every night; the moon died there every morning. Her reluctance to go had come from the fear of leaving the familiar country, the land she knew, but it had become unavoidable. The time for backtracking and evasion had come, escaping into the desert country.

When the moon rose, she too rose and licked the young dog awake. They began to lope towards the fine meeka rising. Black sky. Crisp horns of a quarter; an ancient weeping for Venus in attendance.

They kept running until it was above them and then they stopped and rested for an hour and rose and began to run again. Her thirst was testing her; the young red dog ran beside her, his strength growing. The wound in his back leg all but healed. After all it been just a grazing wound through the meat on the point of the buttock and now he ran with almost full use of all his legs. Close now as he sensed her waning strength; his shoulder to her shoulder to lift her up and continue on their way.

She snarled at him often but he was untroubled by her irritation. His devotion, like his growing stamina, did not waver. His burnt whisker-less face, showing only endurance. She glanced at the ugly blackened snout but saw he was there and he always would be. She had begun to sense now he could run strong and sound. Soon, with luck, he could also hunt. Become a male dog. She would mate with him.

They travelled through miles of mallee scrub and karrik smoke bush, blue bush and bush heather. Through sand and gravel and stands of mulga and gimlet. They ran through another emu-breached hole in the long fence and over ridges and salt pans. Along rock-strewn ridges and through gullies. They passed dried waterholes and crossed the tracks of emu and red kangaroo; the spoor of camels, brumbies, wild cattle and once the wreckage of an ancient biplane, burnt and half-buried by drifting sand. They ran and all they could hear was the desert wind and their own breathing and the sound of their running.

At last they stopped; she lay and panted until her chin sagged into the sand. He ran ahead and looked over the next rise. Far away, a campfire. Figures of the walking people moving around and through the light. The great spiral and showers of shooting stars flashing through the black sky.

She watched his reaction, yipped alarm and lifted her head. She rose and crawled forward to the edge of the ridge. Her nose raised and she smelled the walkers, the look-away wanderers, part of the country like the bungurra and yonga. The rocks and ground, the dust they covered themselves with. Older even than everything. The bitch crawled back from the lip of the ridge and lay and began to try to sleep for a while. Knew they must keep a wary distance, but follow their spoor. They would have to be very careful because the walkers would sense them, and call out and allow them affinity to bring them closer and seduce her and eat her fat pups. Laughing tricksters.

The red dog seemed worried by the desert mob and kept running to her and back to the rise where he could see the far-off fire. Their flames blew west on the east wind come out of the centre. Some bits of a chanting song.

She slept, and in the morning they would return to the caves above the freshwater springs.

Painter was in the men's ward of the Gungurra Public Hospital. Bed 12.

'Mate,' Lew said.

Painter looked up from his Bible. Tried to take a deep breath and looked at Lew over his glasses. 'Son. Sit down. Sit down. Good. Jesus, good to see you boy.' He took off his spectacles. 'Finally got the glasses.'

Lew was holding a bag of grapes. He could hear the wheezing in Painter's chest, the catch and small cough after each breath. He sat down. It hadn't been that long. Maybe a month. Lew sniffed, looked at Painter's emaciated right arm. 'What happened?'

'I came to town and got bad on the drink,' Painter said and lost his breath. He held up a finger. They waited.

'Y'know, after old man Drysdale shot the dogs.'

'You start fightin'?'

'Young Mr McCleod, my you look good boy,' Painter said and coughed. Turned his head to one side and spat into a white enamel bowl. He lay back in the bed. 'What you looking at?'

'You?' Lew looked at Painter as if to ask him, did you hear what I just said?

'Yes I did. It all happened again. Then I was out the monkey.'

'How you now?'

'No good son. No.' Painter coughed. 'Bugger it. Cunt of a thing this. How do I look?'

They were silent. Lew shook his head. 'Not too…y'know. No, not too flash mate. Lost a bit of weight there.'

'It's cancer,' Painter said. 'Jack the Dancer.'

'You sure?'

'Well, they are.' He tried to laugh. 'So there you are.'

'Painter,' Lew said.

'No.'

'All right, you sure?'

'I don't want to talk for a while. Let me get my breath here.' He closed his eyes.

Lew got up, went to find a nurse to ask where the toilets were.

When he returned Painter had woken. 'My young mate the idiot,' he said. 'You ever heard of Hank Williams?' The Bible sitting open on his chest. Spine up, pages down, like spread wings.

'Yep.' Lew sat. He pointed at Painter's chest. 'You reading your Bible mate?'

'You got one?'

'No.'

Painter nodded. 'You can have mine.'

'That's all right.'

'You take it.'

Lew shook his head.

'I can't read son,' Painter said, holding the Bible up and pointing his finger into the pages. 'Never could. All that time.'

Lew stared at the old man lying on the bed like a broken shape. He recognised the tattoos and the voice but that was about all. 'Doesn't matter.'

'How's Drysdale's daughter?' Painter coughed. 'That Clara girl?'

Lew studied the old man. 'I love her.'

Painter closed his eyes and repeated what Lew had said. 'You love her. I saw trouble that day. You passin' nyarnyee up to her when she on that horse, like you passin' a baby to her.' He coughed and spat. 'That was the future I saw Lew. Trouble and no doubt about it.'

Lew stared at the linoleum floor. Painter had begun to ramble. Like he was drunk.

'You talkin' shit Painter.'

'Bastard of a thing that old man did out there boy, Winjilla. There was not even burials. Mad when he come back.'

'It was the best day of my life Painter. The day I knew.'

'Knew?'

'Knew who she was. I was. She, me.'

'No…no I was not talkin' about that. You and her swimming is all Jimmy said. Like that.' Painter made the sign of a middle finger going in and out between the thumb and index finger of the other hand. 'He should not have done that son.'

'No,' Lew said.

'Oh Jesus,' Painter said. 'Old man Drysdale and Dingo

Smith cleaned them up and made a bonfire with what was left. All dead, nortj.' He coughed, leaned over and coughed again as if he would never stop. Dry-retched and raised a trembling hand. 'Never lay a finger on her in anger will you now?' he said.

'I don't know how you could.'

'Well there is a lot you don't know son. About a lot.' Spat spooling blood into a stainless steel bowl.

Lew stared at him. 'Now is not the time to be telling me off again.'

Painter leaned back and held the Bible on his chest. Closed his eyes. 'Not a bloody finger.'

'Mate,' Lew looked at the pale walls of the ward. There were three other beds, separated by curtains. A ceiling fan was circling above them and the edges of some of the curtains moved. The smell of disinfectant and floor cleaner. Green and black linoleum beneath his feet. A white enamel bottle under the bed with a handle and a long neck for Painter to piss into. 'I don't know Painter,' he said. 'I don't know.'

He must have said it a few times because after a while Painter said, 'You can shut up now son don't need to keep saying the same thing over again.'

Coughed and again dry-retched, breathless. 'Over and over you repeating yourself. It's embarrassing. You got shoes on?'

'Yeah mate I got shoes on. Boots.'

'Good. Bout time, you'll be a boss cocky soon. Mr McCleod.' Said his name like he used to. Owner of a winner.

Lew looked at a jug of water and a glass on the bedside table. 'You want anything? Right for smokes? Tobacco? I can bring you whisky if you want. Brandy.'

Painter shook his head and waited. 'Got a spare set of lungs? Another heart? Liver? They all fucked son.'

'Cut it out.'

'Tell me who won the Melbourne Cup?'

'Evening Peal won the Cup; Redcraze second. Dunno who third. Little Georgie Podmore the hoop.'

'Evening Peal,' Painter wheezed. Both hands came around onto the Bible.

'First mare since Rainbird.'

'I would've backed Redcraze myself.'

'Top weight but, ten stone three.'

'That old truck of yours got more rattles than a millionaire's baby son.'

Lew laughed. 'It did.'

'One of the headlights didn't work neither since that little grey roo broke it. Blind in one eye.' Painter was looking towards where the curtain was moving from the motion of the fan. 'Good soup, her tail.'

Lew watched his feet.

'I give it away son,' Painter coughed. 'Our truck. The old Ford.'

'That's all right mate.'

Painter nodded as if confirming what he had known about Lewis McCleod all his life. 'Give it away to a blackfella. Looked like he needed it more than me.'

'Yeah mate. Good.'

'You eat yet?' Painter's eyes opened wide and he looked to where they would bring food.

'No.'

They watched the light easing out of the day from a north-facing window.

The lights came on in the corridor outside the room. Someone was pushing a trolley and Lew smelled reheated mutton and gravy and potatoes, cabbage. One of the other men in the room had turned on his bedside light and a radio was softly playing, Don't Let the Stars Get in Your Eyes.

Painter sighed. He tried to say something else but his voice faded on the words. He remained silent for a very long time then. The sound of his breathing.

'How many pro fights you have, Painter?' Lew whispered. 'You old charcoal burner you?'

No reply. It was like he had fallen asleep. One tattooed hand on the back of the Bible. Thin, skinned knuckles healing over and his knee still propped up. His eyes in shadow and bottom lip jutting.

Lew stood and leaned forward. He couldn't see properly. His hands felt about on Painter's face. Felt the broken nose and cheeks and mouth. All still now. Held his hand. Hand like a broken foot, he would say. Don't sorry me mate. It was like to become paperbark, his face, his voice, such familiar words, all still. Gone.

Rain on the windscreen of the truck and he sat back in his chair. Leaned forward and put his elbows on his knees, looked down and said, 'Painter.' Said it again.

Then he closed his eyes and shook his head. The radio was still playing.

The big homestead kitchen was filled with the smell of baking. Jimmy had his back to the door as she quietly let herself in. He had a radio turned up loud and was singing in Chinese to the Perry Como song. Don't Let the Stars Get in Your Eyes.

The border collie bitch Dee was lying in a kindling box. Jimmy had emptied the box and folded an old horse blanket into the bottom of it. She was curled head to tail and did not look up as Clara entered the kitchen. Her tail gave tight wags and a wave of shivers came over her at the sound of the door. The yonga Gwen was lying on a seagrass mat, also near the fireplace. She had grown and no longer wore a straw hat. When she saw Clara, she stood, leaned forward onto her front feet and then manoeuvred her two large back feet and tail to move closer as she sat quietly and gently at the long table. Jimmy still had his back to her and continued singing.

Gwen scratched at the pocket of Clara's trousers. That was where she kept the barley sugars she would feed to the horses.

Clara fondled the top of Gwen's head and behind her ears. Let her sniff her open hand while looking at the dog. 'Dee,' she whispered. 'Come on now honey, who is the good girl now?'

Dee did not look up but her tail moved a little faster.

'Dee the good girl.' Clara, pursed lips, whistled softly to her. Dee raised her head and opened and closed her mouth. Her wet eyes darted left and right and then back to Clara.

Jimmy remained oblivious, kneading bread, singing.

'Jimmy,' she said and cleared her throat.

Dee half-stood and lowered her head, licked her nose and lowered her chin onto the floor.

'Jimmy.' Louder.

He spun around, bread dough in his hands. *'Ayo tahi suci,* holy shit Miss Clara you give me heart attack isn't it.' He turned the radio off.

Dee had curled up again in the box, but her head was up, eyes glancing and her tail wagged properly.

Jimmy came to the table and stood before her. His flour-covered fingers on the table top. 'I am so pleased. Miss Clara,' he said. 'You come down here again.'

'I had to come, didn't I Jimmy?'

'Yes Miss Clara.'

He fed her with bread and butter and jam. Sweet tea. 'Miss Clara,' he said again as he served her. Slicing the steaming bread. 'Tastes good isn't it?'

As he poured her a cup of tea, he frowned and spoke to her. 'That Pearl,' Jimmy said, 'she is close to having baby foal?'

Clara looked at him. 'Why do you say that, Jimmy?'

He began to butter yet another slice of bread. 'Her *puki* come down, getting big and…dropping. Drooping? She close I think.'

'Her backside, in behind?' Clara asked. 'She is springing?'

He nodded. 'Yes *puki* bouncing up and down when she walk and water coming out not piss. Y'know?'

Clara stood and brushed crumbs off her lap. 'I had better get to her,' she said.

Jimmy clapped his hands. 'Your father, Mr John he…'

She turned and pointed. 'I will not speak of him Jimmy. Understand? Not now. We will not speak of him now.'

'Yes Miss Clara.'

'You hear me?'

'Yes Miss Clara.'

Dee sat up in the box and watched her as she closed the door.

Clara walked out of the homestead kitchen and made her way towards the stables. Tom raised his head as she neared and gave his soft sound of recognition. She walked to him and held his head and spoke to him. The horse took her in with his nostrils, wide-breathing her smell deep into his lungs.

'Now where is our darling Pearl?' she whispered.

Clara crossed the yard and entered the stall and saw Pearl standing in a corner, her sides bulging; looking sad and distracted. She was facing Clara and looked up when she came in. Stamped a front foot as a fly landed on her shoulder, a muscle shivered. Clara walked to her and held her. Pearl too smelled her and then flicked her head at the fly, which had landed on her rump.

'You the big fat girl, come on now let's have a look at you honey,' Clara cooed and took hold of Pearl's tail and pulled her around. Pearl's water had already broken and the feet of a foal were showing. Clara scuffed a boot across the hard clay and sawdust. 'Hold on darling girl,' she said and walked out of the box and found a stack of wheat-straw bales. She carried one back into the box, broke it open and spread the straw over the ground. Repeated this five more times and when she had finished, placed a hand on Pearl's neck, fingers in her mane. 'Go on now.'

Pearl pawed at the straw, sniffed it, circled twice and knelt, waited and then slowly allowed her weight onto her near side, gave a great sigh and rolled over onto her off side. Clara stood back and watched Pearl's belly contract; more fluid accompanied the foal's head as it emerged. It was covered in a gauze-like shroud.

Pearl continued to push, her back off leg lifting with each effort. Clara saw the flushed udder and two black nipples swaying with each contraction. Pearl's breathing rasped as she pushed. She waited, rested and began to get up, knelt, her head going down with her nose touching the ground, blowing air out her nostrils and then, accepting her situation, she lay back down and continued to push. She struggled and the foal's neck and shoulders came out further with wet sucking sounds, it was close now, and then with a final muscular push the seemingly enormous black body of the newborn slid out of her. A gush of uterine fluid washed out over the foal and he was in the world.

Almost immediately he began to throw his head and neck while Pearl's nostrils distended and she looked back at her foal with savage eyes, as wild and profound an animal as Clara had ever seen.

She watched the foal's efforts for a moment and then stepped forward, to clear the white membrane off his head. Both mother and baby seemed to rest. Pause, and think. Some time passed like this. They were both exhausted.

'Oh, the good girl,' Clara said and she felt a shiver run up the back of her neck and across her shoulders.

The mare swung her head around again to smell her newborn and began to position her front feet under herself to stand. Careful, aware of the foal, she rose to her feet and turned to lick off the remaining gauze and blood and matter. As she licked him, the foal suddenly put out a long front leg, started and put out another. His little head swaying and he twitched and all the time Pearl was patiently cleaning him and urging him to rise. His neck becoming stronger, eyes brightening as he listened to his mother's feet moving in the straw. Shook his little head. Alive. Gathered his legs under him and stood, staggered, swayed and tumbled over backwards.

Clara laughed at this most tender of sights, put her hand to her mouth as if to weep; she had no idea how much time had passed. A moment or two, five, fifteen minutes. A newborn standing, staggering, falling and desperate somehow to keep trying. Pearl came to her foal, some of the white shroud and after-birth still swinging from her vulva. Made an ancient throat and belly noise of recognition. Using her nose and face, she lifted and gently urged him to stand. The foal seemed to nod and steady. He swayed and found his feet. And, after a moment, began to search for her teats beneath her front shoulder. Pearl guided him as he kept smelling along her belly until he found her milk. He somehow knew to bend his head, turn it slightly, open his mouth and begin to suckle.

Tears were streaming down Clara's face and she was laughing.

It was early evening when Lew parked the Land Rover in a dry creek bed about half a mile from Daybreak Springs.

A pack on his back, he carried the twelve gauge Remington shotgun in one hand and the Lee Enfield rifle in the other. Long shadows across the land as he made his way to the scrub-covered crest above the waterfall. It was the location he had found and prepared the previous week. He lifted the scrub from the hollow and lay down. Took off his hat. Studied the country stretching out below him. Hollows and lees, flat rocks on which to stand. Approach tracks to the water and the places animals and birds came to drink.

The long pool where they had swum was in darkness. He waited for a while and prepared a firing position. Laid the rifle out, sighted it, opened the bolt, and pushed a magazine into place with an oiled click. Closed the bolt, sliding the brass round into the breach. The .303 was loaded. He made sure the safety catch was off and it was ready.

Lew sat with his back to a gimlet tree and watched the sun setting in the west. A dark red semi-circle and black land for as far as you could see. The air was becoming cold and clean as the desert night closed over him. He leaned forward and touched the rifle. There was a slight dew on the breech block and it felt cold. Thought, I will not think of you old man.

Great black shoulders the boulders. He could hear the scurries of the night creatures. Rock wallabies, woylies. Birds flew to their night perch. And the stars were as if God was showing off. Painter had said would you look at them? Babies hiding in an old woman's hair.

He knew the dingo would come tomorrow. Lay down in the dirt hollow and pulled a thin blanket over his shoulder, thought about Clara. Her smile and approval. How her mouth felt as she kissed him.

The den was warm and dry and the dingo bitch had whelped in the sand. Eaten the placenta and had begun to suckle the three pups that remained alive.

She had taken the three stillborn and left them near the entrance to the den. Carried them gently as she would a live mewling pup, by the tiny scruff. Laid them out, little curled feet and closed eyes: for the black crows. As a gift to the hated black waahdong dog crows who had followed her all her life. This was an offering and her kind would be in them now as they ever shadowed her and her offspring. The rotation of their black wings as they flapped away with her dead pups in their triumphant mouths. Dark shapes in the blue sky.

She had denned near the water below the cave. White gum and paperbark. Tall reeds and spear grass. The comings and goings of zebra finch. Wallaby come down from the rocks to water and once a mob of swift, hard-eyed desert kangaroo come in slowly too. Big sandy boomers overlooking their clan, the dangerous wide-shouldered fighters. Lifted chins.

The young red dog had gone to hunt. He stayed away for a day and a half and returned as the sun was setting. He carried the partial gut and spine of a young rock wallaby; laid it at the entrance to the cave and retreated to watch and listen to the world from the place they had found for her to give birth. He knew he would mate with her soon. He had, as she had taught him, begun to cut large circling tracks from where they were. To stop and wait. To listen and smell the country. Notice what had changed. To allow the hunt to come and to be there when it came. To distrust everything and at the killing, to act and take what was needed to be taken. She had showed him and he had begun to grow with confidence in such instruction. His ears were forward and his mouth open, panting as he watched the world. The burnt whiskers had grown back and he had become a strong and beautiful male dog.

She lay and sighed. Panted as the pups found her teats and bunted at them. The milk came down and flushed through her. Helpless, an arched throat, she looked away as they fed. Courage to feed your young like this. There were more than enough teats now with only three pups. They would be fat. Already they were warm and round and hungry.

She heard a shot coming from a long way off. The red dog hunted in that direction. Two more.

It was early morning when Lew saw the dingo coming down the slope of a rock-filled gully. He saw the liquid working of the dog's shoulders beneath the red fur, how his back feet and tail slowed and balanced his descent, his long tongue, yellow eyes and moving ears. Lew watched as he paused and waited, looked about and raised his nose. How cautious he was, his ability in this land. There was a beautiful silence about him as he made his way down to the water.

When the .303 took him, he lifted both front feet off the ground and spun. Fell over. Got up and tried to run, staggered sideways and fell down again. Cried out at his awful wound.

Lew saw his courage. Blood spurting from his mouth almost like fire. Back legs working, tail out. Old burns along his back. Shot through the chest yet still trying to run.

Lew knew now the direction of the cave where the bitch would have whelped. Where she and the pups would be. The red dingo, trying to get back to her as he died. What else would he do?

The youngster had not come back for a week. She had fed on the remainder of the carcass he had brought to the cave but soon she would have to hunt.

Her three blue-eyed pups sat in the sun and looked at the blinding immensity of the world. Then they began to squeal and whine for milk. Rolled over into their furred selves and pretended to bite. The bitch stepped over them and walked to a flat piece of ground below the den with a good view of the country beneath.

The three mottled pups began to bumble towards the presence of their mother. She looked to where the young red dog would bring meat and lay down and presented her belly to her whelp. The pups ran to bury themselves into her teats.

She opened and closed her mouth a few times but her eyes did not leave the country below them. The hunting country. The ancient lines of her coming to be here and she lay, and knew. Allowed her head back, throat exposed, content with this moment.

She looked up as the light was blocked and his darkness, like a cloud, moved over them.

She did not see the features of the young man. She had not heard him, smelled him. She did not hear the shots.

When Clara saw him again he stood still and she walked to him.

'Lewis.'

'I have brought you these,' he said.

She looked at the sack he was carrying. The tiny pups were moving around in it. Their mewling sounds high pitched.

'They will be hungry.'

'They will,' he said.

She put her arms around him and he felt her fingers, each one of them, on his back.

'Thank you.'

Her breathing and the beating of her heart were loud against his chest, and after a moment, they began to coincide with his.

ACKNOWLEDGMENTS

To Lyn Tranter, an extraordinary woman whose guidance, patience, belief and forthrightness are without equal.

Coming Rain is published *because* of her. My deepest respect and thanks.

Also many thanks to UWA for their support during a very difficult time in 2011.